PAYBACK AT
BLACK VALLEY FORGE

In Sagegrease, John Mitchum arrives straight into a heap of trouble. Someone is stalking him. To get some answers he must ride the long trail to Black Valley and towards his own past. The race is on, and he's up against Turkey Joe Mulligan and his vicious gang of outlaws. But there are others with a stake in the outcome: the rich owner of the Quarter Circle Bucket and the mysterious stranger Challoner. It's payback time for somebody, but who?

EMMETT STONE

PAYBACK AT BLACK VALLEY FORGE

Complete and Unabridged

LINFORD
Leicester

First published in Great Britain in 2011 by
Robert Hale Limited
London

First Linford Edition
published 2013
by arrangement with
Robert Hale Limited
London

British Library CIP Data

Stone, Emmett.
    Payback at Black Valley Forge. - -
(Linford western library)
1. Western stories.
2. Large type books.
I. Title II. Series
823.9'2–dc23

ISBN 978–1–4448–1492–7

Published by
F. A. Thorpe (Publishing)
Anstey, Leicestershire

Set by Words & Graphics Ltd.
Anstey, Leicestershire
Printed and bound in Great Britain by
T. J. International Ltd., Padstow, Cornwall

This book is printed on acid-free paper

1

Outside the saloon a lot of yelling and shouting was taking place but it was good humoured. Jess Stevens, the town marshal, leaned against a stanchion and watched the cowpokes having a good time. They had just sold the herd of cattle they had driven up from the Gulf country and were blowing their hard-earned wages on drink, gambling and girls. It made for good business; any town like Sagegrease stood to benefit if it wasn't razed to the ground in the process. He had seen a few cow towns come and go — Baxter Springs, Ellsworth, Cheyenne. The thing to worry about was not the activities of cowboys at trail's end but the extension of the railroad to a new cattle trail terminus. Sagegrease was enjoying its brief spell in the sun. It would be nice to think it might survive, but it would take some effort.

The uproar became louder as the batwings swung open and a tall, thin figure emerged. Stevens observed him more closely. There was something about him which seemed different from the rest of the cowhands and it had nothing to do with his general appearance. He wore the usual soiled range clothes and Stetson hat. It was more to do with the way the rest of the men regarded him, quietening their antics to acknowledge him with a nod, moving aside to let him pass down the boardwalk. He strolled as far as the grocery store and went inside. After a few moments the door opened and was held ajar by the man as a lady Stevens recognized as Lucy Wetherall came out carrying some bags. The man closed the door gently and lifted his hat in acknowledgement of something she said to him. He carried another big bag and placed it carefully in a buggy drawn up by the boardwalk. Then he turned away, walking back to the Legal

Tender and stepping down to unfasten his horse, a big Appaloosa, from the hitchrack. At the same moment the batwings swung open and two men appeared. They stepped down from the boardwalk and continued moving away from him, fanning out as they did so. Suddenly one of them turned.

'Mitchum!'

The sound of his voice was harsh and seemed to cut across the other noises like a wedge separating what had gone before from what was about to happen next. The man addressed as Mitchum didn't turn but continued to stand with his back to them.

'I called your name,' the man said.

There was no response from Mitchum. Even now the marshal hadn't registered that anything untoward was taking place.

'Mitchum, you're a two-bit cowardly prairie dog.'

Very slowly, Mitchum began to turn. At these last words the marshal started from his lethargy. He looked closely at the men but didn't recognize them. It seemed unlikely they were part of the Gulf country outfit.

'I'm callin' you, Mitchum. Some folk say you're quick. I say you're a washed out piece of buffalo dung.'

The marshal took a step away from the stanchion. At the same instant he saw the man who had accosted Mitchum go for his gun. Mitchum was sideways on to both men and it seemed he could not have seen the man's hand drop to his holster, but before the man had his gun in his hand, Mitchum's revolver was drilling hot lead into his chest. The other man had drawn his weapon and his finger was on the trigger as Mitchum spun and fired again. The two guns went off simultaneously. For a moment both men stood as if transfixed, looking at one another. The street seemed oddly silent after the crash of gunfire; gun-smoke hung like a gauze curtain between the two combatants. A number of people had emerged from the stores lining the street, watching the scene from a distance with shocked attention. Another

4

instant of time went past with leaden feet. The two men still stood immobile but then the marshal saw blood running down the face of the man whose companion lay in a crumpled heap in the dirt. The man was looking at Mitchum with a puzzled look and then without warning he toppled forward like a felled log. Mitchum remained still for just another instant and then he stepped forward a few paces and looked down at his two assailants. He put his gun back into its holster and looked up to where the marshal was approaching.

'Didn't want to have to do it,' he said. 'They gave me no choice.'

'I saw it,' the marshal replied.

Mitchum reached into a pocket and produced a couple of silver coins.

'Give that to the undertaker,' he said.

The marshal kneeled down to examine the two dead bodies.

'Do you know who these men are?' he said.

'Nope. Ain't made their acquaintance.'

Mitchum turned and walked back to his horse. Some of his fellows from the saloon had gathered round and one of them patted him on the back. He finished untying the horse and stepped into leather. He turned and nodded at some of the roistering cowboys. Someone shouted:

'Good luck, Mr Mitchum!'

Stevens noted the respectful tone of the address. The stranger touched the horse lightly with his spurs and it moved off slowly down the street.

Mitchum kept on riding till he was a long way from town. The sun was sinking low when he finally stopped to set up camp in a spot formed by a bend in a stream, framed by willows and cottonwood trees. He tended to the Appaloosa and then set about making himself comfortable, building a fire and laying slabs of bacon in a pan. By the time he had eaten, the moon had climbed high; he pulled out a pouch of tobacco and rolled himself a cigarette. A gentle breeze blew down from the hills and he felt refreshed. He had money in his pocket from the cattle drive and time on his hands. He had got along well with the rest of the men on the trail but he felt distanced from most of them. Maybe it was his age. They had urged him to ride back with them to the Apple Bar but he wanted a change. A change to what he didn't know. He didn't intend wasting any effort thinking about it.

He awoke in the small hours. In an instant he was alert and his gun was in his hand. He had moved back from the fire to where he had a view of the clearing. The last embers had died away but he could see enough by the light of the stars. Nearby, the whisper of the running stream and the soughing of the wind in the trees was the only sound to disturb the stillness of the night. From a little way off his horse stamped and snorted. He listened intently and caught the faint rhythm of horses' hoofs. It carried on the wind for a few moments and then vanished away. For a while longer he sat up and then he lay down again and closed his eyes. When he opened them it was dawn.

He got up and made his way to the pool. He took off his clothes and dived in. The water was cold and when he came out his skin was tingling. He dressed and then relit the fire. It was while he was eating that he heard the sound of hoofs but he wasn't concerned. He had been half expecting to have visitors. After a time a voice called out and then a couple of the Apple Bar boys rode into the clearing accompanied by a third man who wore a star.

'Howdy,' Mitchum greeted them. 'Guess you could do with some coffee.' The ranch-hands looked grim. The three riders swung down from their saddles and joined him by the fire.

'I got a feelin' that what you're about to tell me ain't gonna be good,' Mitchum said.

The cowpunchers looked to the marshal.

'OK,' he said. 'I don't intend beatin'

about the bush.'

He turned to Mitchum.

'I don't know if this has anythin' to do with what happened yesterday. After you left, the rest of the boys were enjoyin' themselves and things got a bit colourful. To cut a long story short, there was trouble. A fight broke out.'

Mitchum looked at the two Apple Bar riders.

'That ain't all,' one of them said.

'Seems like your boys upset a bunch of cowboys from the Quarter Circle Bucket. That's a big spread to the north of town. Your boys came off best. Trouble is, seems the Quarter Circle men weren't prepared to leave it at that.'

The marshal looked towards the two men from the Apple Bar, Bill Casper and Ron Murray. They were good cowhands.

'They bushwhacked a couple of us on their way back to camp. Shot 'em down in cold blood,' Casper said.

Mitchum was suddenly attentive.

'Yeah,' he said. 'Who?'

'Clint Darcy and Ron Hayes.'

Mitchum's mouth set in a grim line.

'I know you finished your business with the Apple Bar,' Murray added. 'But we all figured you'd want to know.'

Mitchum got to his feet.

'Appreciate it,' he said.

He turned to the marshal.

'What's your role in this?'

'I'm ridin' on over to the Quarter Circle right now,' the marshal replied.

'You get on back,' Mitchum said to the other two. 'There ain't nothin' more you can do.'

They started to expostulate but Mitchum cut them short.

'This don't involve you any further,' he said. 'Best thing you can do is get on back to the Apple Bar.'

'What about you, Mr Mitchum?' Murray inquired.

Mitchum took a moment to consider.

'I'm goin' with the marshal,' he said.

The marshal merely nodded his head.

'Sure,' he replied.

The Apple Bar riders were still reluctant but didn't stop to argue the matter any further. With a final word of farewell they swung into leather and rode away.

'Guess I'd better introduce myself properly,' the marshal said when they had disappeared from sight. 'Name's Stevens, Jess Stevens.'

'Mitchum, John Mitchum.'

The marshal looked closely at him and was thoughtful.

'You wouldn't be the same John Mitchum tamed Red Rock?' he said.

The suggestion of a smile lifted the corner of Mitchum's mouth.

'Some might say that,' he said. 'I'd say things just quieted down some.'

'Didn't stay that way,' Stevens said. 'Not after you left.'

Mitchum shrugged.

'I don't know,' he replied. 'I never went back.'

The marshal decided to turn the conversation in a different direction.

'Sure happy to have you along,' he said, 'but do you mind if I ask one question: why?'

'Ron Hayes was my deputy in Red Rock. We rode a few trails together before and since. He was ramroddin' the cattle drive. It was him who asked me if I wanted to come along. Guess I'm just returnin' the favour.'

There were a few other things the marshal would have liked to ask but he decided to leave it.

They were riding towards the hills. As they rode Marshal Stevens filled Mitchum in with some details about the ranch.

'Those hills is full of mustangs,' he said. 'Old Sam Bucket saw the potential for some horse-breedin'.'

'Never figured mustangs were much use as cow ponies.'

'Maybe not. I guess hosses is just as different as folks.'

'So he rounds 'em up and breaks 'em in. Can't be a lot of money in that.'

'I guess it's more of a hobby. Sam don't need to concern himself about money. He made his pile; don't ask me how. He just enjoys playin' the role of big rancher.'

'Does he spend a lot of time away?'

'Used to. He's kind of retired now. Wait till you see the place. Imported furniture, the best wine and whiskey, paintin's.'

'You figure we'll get that far?'

'Big Sam is OK,' the marshal replied. 'That's why it seems kinda strange that any of his boys would get involved in a shootin' affair.'

Mitchum did not reply. Instead he looked up towards a ridge where he had just seen a flash of light. Before he could utter a word of warning, there came a puff of smoke followed by the crump of a bullet and Mitchum felt a stab of pain as the shot ripped into his shoulder. Neither man hesitated; in a second they had slid from the saddle and pulled their horses to the ground. A second shot rang out and tore up dust nearby. Mitchum had his rifle to his shoulder and fired in the direction of the smoke curling into the air above them. Stevens did the same. Mitchum's eyes scanned the hillside.

'Seems like there's only one of 'em,' he said.

'Are you OK?' Stevens asked.

Mitchum looked down at the blood oozing from his shoulder.

'Yeah. It's only a flesh wound. Nothin' seems to be broken.'

They were expecting more shots but none came. Then, from somewhere on the opposite side of the hill, they heard the sound of hoofs.

'Looks like he's decided to call it a day,' Mitchum said.

They waited a few moments longer and then stood up, raising their horses.

'Let's take a look,' the marshal said.

They mounted and rode up to the spot where they reckoned the gunman had been concealed. There were scuffs in the soil where the gunman's boots had trod and, further back, the imprints of hoofs. The marshal returned to the spot where the gunman had been situated and commenced to look more closely. After a while he shouted to Mitchum and held something up.

'A cartridge case!' he called.

Mitchum rode up. Together, he and the marshal examined it.

'.50 calibre,' Mitchum said. 'Nothin' unusual there.'

'Remington. A favourite with sharp-shooters.'

'He weren't so sharp,' Mitchum said. 'He only grazed me.'

The marshal looked thoughtful.

'Less'n it was meant as some kinda warnin'.'

'For me or for you?' Mitchum said.

'It was you he hit,' the marshal replied. 'I don't figure he was that bad a marksman.'

When Stevens had cleaned Mitchum's wound with water from his flask and bound it with their bandannas, they mounted and rode on.

Stevens was right about the Quarter Circle Bucket; even from the outside it presented a grand appearance. It wasn't like anything that Mitchum had ever seen before. The ranch house was long and high and rambling, with a variety of excrescences and additions. Verandas and covered passageways linked the main building with a number of others. Windows were not flat but projected. If Mitchum had known anything about architecture, he might have recognized it as belonging to the American Bracketed style, but he didn't. It just seemed an extraordinary thing to find near a place like Sagegrease.

'What did I tell you?' the marshal said. 'Ever seen anythin' like it?'

They rode on past some outlying buildings of a more conventional type into what passed as the yard, where they dismounted and tied their horses to the hitching rail. As they did so the door of the ranch house opened and a man appeared who, in his own way, seemed as eccentric and unlikely as the house. He was well built but his whole frame appeared to be twisted to one side. His hair was white and hung in untidy locks to his shoulders, but his white beard, by contrast, was cut short and carefully trimmed. He was smoking a pipe of a kind Mitchum had not seen before. It was a calabash pipe with a meerschaum bowl carved into an elaborate design which seemed to include horses. Over the years the white meerschaum had matured into a warm golden brown colour. As he advanced along the wide veranda, the man seemed to walk with a distinctive roll.

'Marshal Stevens! Good to see you again.'

He paused to look at Mitchum.

'Good to find you lookin' well,' the marshal replied. 'This here is John Mitchum.'

He waited while Mitchum and Bucket exchanged nods before adding:

'He used to ride with an outfit called the Apple Bar.'

The marshal, like Mitchum, was observing the old man carefully but there was no sign of a response.

'The Apple Bar hit town lately with a herd of beefs.'

Bucket returned Mitchum's gaze.

'Yeah? Hope he got a good price for 'em.'

'We got a fair price,' Mitchum replied.

Bucket reached into a pocket of his jacket to produce a tamper with which he pressed down on his pipe. The aroma of the tobacco hung in the air with a distinctive fruity tang.

'Come on in,' the rancher said when he had finished. 'Guess you must be thirsty after ridin' the trail.'

He stood back while Mitchum and the marshal entered. The inside of the house was almost as remarkable as the outside. It wasn't a particularly large room but still gave an unusual impression of spaciousness. Mitchum couldn't at first see why this was the case and then it struck him that the room was devoid of the usual clutter of furniture. Instead there were only a few chairs, a settee and a table which seemed marooned in a sea of wood flooring on which, here and there, a few expensive rugs had been tossed in an apparently casual but in fact calculated fashion. There was a large, heavy chandelier and a cabinet containing bottles and glasses. Bucket walked over to the cabinet.

'Brandy, gentlemen?'

When Mitchum tasted it even his unpractised pallet could discern its quality.

'Armagnac,' Bucket continued, 'imported from France. They say it has therapeutic qualities. One claim is that it restores the memory. That's all I have left now.'

'That ain't true,' the marshal replied. 'After all, you got this place.'

'Yes, I have the Quarter Circle. That should be more than enough.'

For a moment there was silence while they enjoyed the taste of the brandy.

'Well,' Bucket eventually resumed, 'I don't suppose you gentlemen rode out here for fun. I suppose the matter has something to do with the Apple Bar which you referred to just now. How can I be of help?'

Stevens had to make an almost conscious effort to get back to business.

'I'm investigatin' a couple of shootin's. Both victims were Apple Bar employees. One of them was a particular friend of Mr Mitchum.'

He turned to Mitchum as if for confirmation but Mitchum remained silent.

'How does this concern me?' Bucket asked.

'Shortly before the incident took place, there was some trouble between the Apple Bar men and some boys from the Quarter Circle Bucket.'

'What? You think that could have led to the shootings?'

'Seems like a reasonable hypothesis.'

'A hypothesis is all it remains, and not a very good one. I can assure you that none of my men was concerned in these killings.'

'How can you be so sure?' Mitchum interpolated.

'Because I know them too well. Sure,

they might get a bit rowdy occasionally, but they wouldn't get involved in that sort of behaviour.'

There was an awkward atmosphere in the room.

'Would you mind if I had a word with your foreman? He would know just who was in town on Friday night,' Stevens said.

'I can tell you that myself.'

'OK. So there would be no objection to me seein' them?'

'There certainly would be. I'm afraid you're barking up the wrong tree, Marshal.'

Mitchum finished his drink and put the glass down.

'Sorry to have bothered you, Mr Bucket,' he said. 'Sure appreciate the brandy.'

He glanced in the direction of Stevens.

'Thanks for the drink,' Stevens began. 'If you . . . '

He stopped when he saw the steely glint in Bucket's eyes. He might be courteous but he was as likely to yield as flint. The marshal followed Mitchum outside and they mounted up.

'Nice to see you, boys,' Bucket said. 'Hope you get this thing sorted out.'

Stevens touched his hand to the brim of his Stetson and then he and Mitchum rode out of the yard.

'Didn't get much out of him,' Stevens said. 'Guess I'll have to come back with a warrant.'

'Don't bother,' Mitchum said. 'He can't tell us nothin'.'

'Why do you say that?'

'Because neither him nor any of his men had anythin' to do with it.'

The marshal was silent for a moment.

'Better get you to the doc's,' he concluded.

Doctor Robertson confirmed what Mitchum had said; that the wound was not serious. Still, it was painful and would put Mitchum out of action for a day or two.

'You need to rest it; take it easy.'

'Reckon I'd best check in at the nearest hotel,' Mitchum said. 'What do you suggest?'

'There's only one, the Alhambra,' the doctor said.

'Then I'd best get on over.'

The marshal thought for a moment.

'Reckon you could do with somethin' a little more homely,' he said. 'Why don't you try Lucy Wetherall? Her place might not be as grand as the Alhambra but it's probably a lot more comfortable.'

'Home cookin',' the doctor said. 'Can't be beaten.'

Mitchum looked from one to the other.

'Sure,' he said. 'Just point me in the right direction.'

'I'll take you there,' the marshal said. 'I can make the introductions.'

His thoughts reverted to the previous day when he had seen Mitchum holding open the door of the general store for Lucy Wetherall. It seemed that maybe Mitchum had something of a head start in terms of gaining her approval.

Lucy Wetherall had a medium sized house towards the edge of town, two rooms of which she let out. When the marshal and Mitchum arrived she was hanging some washing which stretched between two trees in her garden.

'Hello, Lucy,' the marshal said. 'Got a visitor for you.'

She looked up and then, realizing she still had a peg in her mouth, blushed slightly as she took it out.

'Howdy,' Mitchum said. 'I believe we met before.'

'Of course,' she replied. 'Aren't you the gentlemen who helped with my purchases at the grocery store?'

Mitchum nodded. There was an awkward silence relieved by the voice of the marshal.

'Mr Mitchum is staying in town for a few days. I was wonderin' how you were fixed for guests?'

'I only have one at the moment,' she replied.

She looked more closely at Mitchum and seemed to notice his bandaged shoulder for the first time.

'Mr Mitchum,' she said, 'have you been hurt?'

'It weren't nothin', ma'am,' he replied.

'Doc Robertson figures it would be sensible for Mr Mitchum to rest it awhile,' the marshal said.

The woman smiled.

'Of course,' she replied. 'You'd be very welcome to stay, Mr Mitchum.'

'Thank you, ma'am.'

'Of course, you'll have to take us as you find us. Nothin' fancy.'

Mitchum wondered whether she was referring to herself and her other guest when she spoke of 'us', but the question was answered when there came sounds of movement within the house followed by a rush of feet and a boy of about twelve came running through the door, rapidly followed by a yellow-brown dog. For an instant Mitchum was reminded of the colour of Bucket's pipe. The boy pulled up at the sight of the marshal and Mitchum but the dog came on and started jumping about Mitchum's feet, barking as it did so. Mitchum bent down and ruffled its fur.

'Looks like you've found a friend there,' the marshal remarked.

'Let me introduce you to my son, Jimmy,' Lucy said. 'And you seem to be already on familiar terms with Rusty.'

Mitchum turned to the boy.

'Does he do any tricks?' he asked.

The boy suddenly became animated.

'Sure does,' he said.

He called to the dog and shouted some instruction. The dog rolled over with its paws in the air.

'He wants you to tickle his tummy,' the boy said.

Mitchum obliged.

'Now watch this,' Jimmy said. 'Rusty, play dead.'

The dog rolled over on its side and lay still.

'That's very impressive,' Mitchum said. 'Maybe we could teach him a few more.'

'Yes, he likes doin' tricks,' the boy responded.

'That's enough botherin' Mr Mitchum for now,' his mother said. 'Go and play while I take Mr Mitchum in the house and show him his room.'

The boy looked at Mitchum.

'Maybe later,' Mitchum said.

The boy and the dog ran off round a corner of the house.

'You mustn't mind Jimmy,' his mother said. 'He can be a bit boisterous at times.'

'Seems a good boy,' Mitchum replied. 'It's good for a boy to have a dog.'

Mitchum was wondering if the boy had a father still around as he and Stevens followed Lucy Wetherall into the house. It was quite large and showed a woman's touch at every turn — lace curtains at the windows, vases of flowers, ornaments and on one sideboard, some faded photographs. One of them showed a man in uniform looking awkwardly at the camera.

'My husband,' Lucy said. 'He was

killed right at the end of the war.'

'I'm real sorry,' Mitchum said. 'I saw some action myself.'

Mitchum's room was upstairs. It was tastefully appointed like the rest of the house and overlooked the back garden. Jimmy's shouts and the occasional barking of the dog came to their ears through the open window. At the back of the house the garden sloped down to a fence beyond which an open meadow stretched to the banks of a stream.

'It's a real nice room,' Stevens said.

Lucy turned to Mitchum.

'Are you sure it will be suitable, Mr Mitchum?' she asked.

'It's just fine,' Mitchum replied. 'Sure appreciate you offerin' to put me up.'

'It's a pleasure,' she said.

They went back downstairs.

'Supper will be ready in about another hour,' Lucy said. 'In the meantime, just make yourself at home.'

'You mentioned you had another guest?' the marshal put in. He liked to know what was going on around town.

'Mr Challoner,' Lucy replied. 'A nice gentleman. He's a drummer. Something to do with Glidden wire, if that means anything to you. He should be back anytime soon.'

Stevens turned and made his way to the door.

'Sure nice talkin' to you, ma'am,' he said. 'Would it be OK if I maybe stop by sometime and see how Mitchum is gettin' along?'

'I think I can manage,' Mitchum said.

'Of course, anytime.'

'Give my regards to Jimmy and the dog.'

The marshal walked away down the path and out of the gate. Mitchum and Lucy watched him till a tree cut off their field of vision. They were standing together on the veranda when Mitchum suddenly became very aware of her presence. Just at that moment the dog came bounding into view and Jimmy appeared round the corner of the house.

'Want to come and throw some sticks?' he shouted.

Mitchum looked down at Lucy and smiled.

'Sure thing,' he replied.

Late that night Mitchum lay on his bed, looking up at the ceiling and thinking about recent events. The drummer had proved to be a dull fellow but what he said was troubling. Mitchum had never heard of Glidden wire. He was familiar with the use of smooth wire to fence in cows; he had put up plenty of wire fences himself. But this was something new. Challoner was enthusiastic. He predicted a revolution in fencing. Of course, it was his job to be keen, but why did it bother Mitchum? Something else was bothering him too. Who had shot him and why? Even from the start, Stevens's theory that the killings of Clint Darcy and Ron Hayes had been at the hands of employees of the Quarter Circle Bucket had seemed to him at least questionable. Now that he had been out to the ranch and met Bucket it made no sense at all. There was something about Bucket that jarred, but it had nothing to do with the killings of Darcy and Hayes. Perhaps his own shooting had been coincidental but he didn't think so. He had ridden with Hayes; Hayes had been his friend, his deputy back in Red Rock. It was too much to imagine that the sequence of events had been accidental. In that case, why had the three of them been targeted? And by whom?

He recalled the sound of those hoof beats in the night as he got up and walked to the window. The night outside was cloudy and starless. From down the stairs the dog barked twice and then was silent again. He reached for his tobacco pouch and rolled himself a smoke. As he inhaled his first lungful he knew the answer. The connection had to be Red Rock. When he and Hayes had tamed that town they had made a lot of enemies. OK, so it was a long time ago. That didn't make any difference, some grudges were never forgotten. Someone from out of the past had tracked them to Sagegrease. Probably more than one. In all likelihood, the slaying of Darcy had been accidental. Hayes had been the target and now he himself was. At any moment a bullet could seek him out from a dark alley, a patch of brush or some rocks on a mountainside. Like that afternoon. The only way to resolve the situation would be to find out who was responsible. Mitchum blew out a cloud of smoke. There was just one other thing he wasn't so sure about. Had the shot which had found him that afternoon been meant to kill? Was it a bad shot or was it some kind of warning? Time would tell.

2

Mitchum had been advised by the doctor to rest up for a few days, but he had no intention of letting that hold him back. The next morning, after breakfast, he made his way to the livery stable to pick up his horse and rode off in the direction of the hills. He wanted to see if he could find any clues that he and the marshal had missed. Besides, it was his habit to familiarize himself with the local terrain. It might come in useful to know the lie of the land. His shoulder hurt and his arm was stiff but it seemed to loosen up once he was on his way.

At first the land was without distinguishing features, a gently rolling plain of short buffalo grass, still green but just beginning to turn a yellow-grey. Then he was among the slopes, with scattered clumps of trees and rocks and streamlets overhung here and there in the hollows with willow and cottonwood. He was being very careful now, although he felt it not very likely that anyone would be there to take another pot-shot at him. He came to the crest of a long rise and saw beneath him to his left the long straight rails of the spur line. Then he saw something else. Lying in the grass some distance away was the figure of a man with a pair of field glasses held to his eyes. The man seemed intent on something and so far was unaware of Mitchum's presence. For a moment Mitchum was about to slip from the saddle and creep up on him, but then he thought better of it and began to ride down the slope towards the prostrate figure. The man continued to look through his field glasses, apparently still oblivious of Mitchum. Only when Mitchum was almost upon him did he turn and, holding the glasses at arm's length, roll on to his side and look up at the new arrival.

'Hello,' he said.

Mitchum was somewhat put out by the man's casual attitude. He showed no sign of surprise or concern. It was as if he had been waiting for Mitchum to arrive and his next words confirmed that impression.

'Saw you from a long ways off. Lost sight of you when you got into the foothills. Wondered if you'd put in an appearance.'

He paused for a moment and then got to his feet.

'Name's Flagg, Zachary Flagg.'

Mitchum dropped from the saddle.

'John Mitchum,' he replied.

By way of reply the man turned his back and pointed to the railroad track.

'Should be a train comin' by real soon,' he said. 'I still can't believe in 'em.'

Mitchum looked at the man more closely. He was an oldster, dry and lined as tree bark and skinny as a stick.

'Like I say, should be a train right soon; and by Jiminy, there she comes.'

He clapped his field glasses to his eyes again. In the distance Mitchum could just perceive a faint smudge which he guessed was smoke from the engine. Almost without realizing what he was doing, he began to watch as the smoke cloud got bigger and the train appeared, crawling slowly across the landscape like an insect. The man handed Mitchum his glasses and Mitchum took them.

'Sure is a sight, ain't it?' the man said.

Mitchum watched the train as it came closer. Behind the engine were the caboose and four carriages. Mitchum had caught some of the oldster's enthusiasm.

'Looks like she's findin' it hard goin',' he said.

The sound of the engine as it ground its way up the gradient reached their ears. It grew steadily louder. Mitchum handed the glasses back to the oldster and continued to watch as the train disappeared round the brow of the hill.

The noise dropped in tone and soon all that was left was a thin trail of smoke billowing in the breeze.

'I know someone who'd enjoy watchin' the train from up here,' Mitchum said.

The oldster raised a questioning eyebrow.

'Young fella name of Jimmy,' Mitchum said.

The oldster's mouth widened in a hollow grin.

'You wouldn't mean young Jimmy Wetherall?' he said.

'Yeah, that's the one. Has a dog named Rusty.'

'Well I'll be a danged . . . Say, does that mean you're stayin' at Lucy Wetherall's place?'

'Just for a few days. Till this arm gets better.'

He felt suddenly embarrassed.

'Doctor's orders,' he added.

The oldster looked at his wound.

'I seen what happened,' he said.

Mitchum didn't show his surprise.

'You saw what happened? You mean,

you saw me get shot?'

'Sure did. Seen it all through these here glasses.'

'What did you see?'

'Like I say, I saw it all. Seen you and the marshal first, from a distance. It was only when you'd got pretty close that I seen the other fella. He was hidin' behind some bushes but I got him in my sights. It was then I seen he had the rifle. Woulda tried to warn you but it was too late.'

'Did you recognize him? Was he local?'

The oldster suddenly spat a thick gob of spittle.

'I lived round these parts most o' my life. Ain't never seen that fella round here before.'

'You sure you got a good look?'

'Perfect. Had to take care not to let him catch any reflection. Lookin' through these things, he was as close as you are to me.'

'What did he look like? Can you describe him?'

'Now there's a thing,' the oldster mused. 'I reckon I most never forget a face but in this case there's no way I could be mistaken.'

He paused, as if for effect. He seemed to be enjoying the interest Mitchum was taking. For a moment Mitchum wondered whether he wasn't putting it on.

'I thought you said you'd never seen him before?' Mitchum said.

'I said I'd never seen him round here.'

'Go on,' Mitchum said.

The oldster drew out the moment just a little longer.

'I couldn't be mistaken,' he said, 'because I've seen the face before one time. On a Wanted poster. That face was the face of Turkey Joe Mulligan.'

'Turkey Joe Mulligan! He's never been seen north of Red River!'

'He has now.'

It only took a minute for it to make sense. Mitchum had crossed swords with Turkey Joe in Red Rock. He had been instrumental once in getting Joe sent to the Penitentiary.

'Never could work out why they called him Turkey,' the oldster remarked inconsequentially.

'Mulligan used to make a livin' one time huntin' turkeys somewhere down in the Cherokee Strip.'

'So it ain't nothin' to do with the way he looks?'

'You tell me. I ain't clapped eyes on him in a long time. Anyway, how did you get up here?'

'Same way as you except I'm ridin' a mule.'

Mitchum looked about.

'I left her at the bottom of the hill,' Flagg said. 'Walked the last bit.'

He turned and then noticed the string of Mitchum's sack of Bull Durham hanging from his shirt pocket.

'Don't suppose you could spare a smoke before you go?' he said.

Mitchum pulled out the pouch and handed it to the oldster.

'Help yourself,' he said. 'Papers are in there.'

When Flagg had finished Mitchum rolled a cigarette. They both sat on the grass.

'Funny thing, ain't it,' the oldster said. 'I mean, the way things change.'

Mitchum wasn't sure what he was referring to but let him run on.

'Take that old iron horse. Wouldn't have believed such a thing possible when I was a boy. Next thing you know folk'll be flyin' through the air like birds.'

Mitchum grunted.

'They'll be flyin' to the moon in some such contraption,' the oldster added. 'Less'n they grow feathers.'

They both chuckled. When he had finished smoking Mitchum got to his feet. The oldster showed no inclination to move.

'Guess I'll be on my way,' Mitchum said. 'Thanks for the information.'

The oldster looked up.

'Woulda told the marshal,' he said.

'When I got the chance.'

'Sure.'

'What'll you do now?' Flagg asked. 'Go after the varmint?'

'Could be a mite difficult to find.'

The oldster paused, taking a long last drag from his cigarette.

'Know that too,' he said.

For a moment his words did not register with Mitchum. Then the import of the man's brief statement hit him.

'What!' he ejaculated. 'You mean you know where Turkey Joe Mulligan is to be found?'

The oldster nodded.

'Pretty sure. He's taken over an old cabin higher up in the hills. I used to make use of it myself sometimes. When I'd be spendin' time up here and in no hurry to get back to Sagegrease. I was there only a few days ago. Knowed straight away there was somethin' wrong. The ground was all scuffed up. There were horse droppings. So I hung about.'

Mitchum rolled another cigarette for Flagg and himself, settling back on the grass beside him, prepared to let the oldster tell it in his own time.

'Had me a long wait,' he continued. 'Almost gave up when who should come ridin' in but Turkey Joe. Of course, I didn't realize it was him straight off. Never got a real good look till I saw him on the hillside takin' aim at you.'

'Then how do you know it was the same man?'

'It was him. I saw enough.'

Mitchum pondered the man's words. Maybe he was all wrong about Turkey Joe. Still, it would be worth while taking a look at that cabin.

'Where is this place?' he said.

'Higher up. Further on. It's kind of difficult to find.'

'Just tell me how to get there,' Mitchum said.

The oldster stroked his stubbled chin.

'Like I say, it's kinda hard to describe.'

43

He jumped up.

'Tell you what,' he said. 'Why don't I show you myself?'

Mitchum didn't know what to say or how to react. He still had a feeling that the oldster was maybe taking him for a fool.

'I got nothin' else to do,' Flagg said. 'If we get movin', we could be there well before sundown.'

Mitchum was in a quandary. A new thought had occurred to him. What if the oldster was not playing him for a fool but was leading him into a trap? What was there to say he wouldn't take him straight to Mulligan? Who was he and what was he really doing up here? Mitchum preferred to ride alone. Just then his cogitations were interrupted by a loud braying and a mule appeared at the bottom of the slope.

'By Jiminy, that's old Jane!' the oldster shouted 'She musta bust loose from where I tied her.'

Without waiting for a reply he began running down the slope with a surprising turn of speed. He was half way down when he suddenly tripped and went tumbling the rest of the way. Mitchum couldn't help but grin as he made his way down to where the oldster was lying. When he reached him the oldster looked dazed and there was a cut across his forehead.

'What happened?' he breathed. 'Somebody take a shot?'

Mitchum's grin broadened.

'Nobody took a shot,' he replied. 'You took a fall.'

Gently, he started to help the old man to his feet when he thought better of it.

'You wait here,' he said. 'I'll catch the mule and then we can both ride back to Sagegrease.'

The oldster was shaken and looked giddy and offered no objections to Mitchum's proposal.

'Wait here,' Mitchum repeated, although he had no expectation that the oldster would do anything different. It didn't take him long to round up both the mule and his own horse. When he got back the oldster was sitting up and Mitchum offered him his flask.

'Whiskey,' he said.

The old man drank and afterwards seemed to have recovered something of his old verve.

'About that cabin . . . ' he began, but Mitchum stopped him with a shake of his head.

'Let's get on back to Sagegrease,' he said. 'The cabin can wait.'

Over supper that night Mitchum broached the subject of Flagg.

'You mean old Zachary Flagg?' Lucy replied. 'Of course you do. There couldn't be two of him.'

She laughed and the drummer looked up as if surprised at her levity.

'Zachary's something of a character. He's been around town as long as anybody can remember. By all accounts he used to be quite an important citizen but somewhere along the line he hit bad times and now he gets by whichever way he can. He helps out at the saloon and the livery stables — folks can usually find something for him to do. He's not above askin' people for a handout.'

She reached across the table for some bread.

'He might have some savings for all I know. Where did you come across him?'

Mitchum told her about his encounter in the hills, but without mentioning anything about Turkey Joe Mulligan.

'I think he spends a lot of time up there,' Lucy said. 'He's quite an interesting person once he gets talking.'

The dog was sitting between Mitchum and young Jimmy and, having first checked that it was OK, Mitchum tossed it a scrap of meat from his plate.

'He's gettin' fat,' Jimmy said.

'Maybe me and you could take him for a walk later,' Mitchum replied.

He turned to the drummer.

'Care to come?' he asked.

'You must excuse me,' Challoner replied. 'I have some paperwork I must attend to tonight.'

Mitchum failed to notice the look of relief on the boy's face.

'I think I might come along too,' Lucy said. 'If you two boys don't mind?'

Whatever Jimmy thought, Mitchum was pleased to have her along. They went down to the river and started walking along the bank. Jimmy and Mitchum threw sticks into the water and the dog splashed in after them. When Jimmy had run off a little way ahead, Lucy turned to Mitchum.

'Jimmy likes you,' she said.

'I like him.'

She paused.

'I hope you don't mind me asking, but did you have a reason for riding up into the hills?'

Mitchum hesitated for a moment but then saw no point in prevaricating.

'I guess it's pretty obvious that someone took a shot at me,' he said. 'I thought I might just find some kinda clue as to who it might be.'

'And did you? Find a clue?

'No,' Mitchum replied. He saw no reason to go into details about his conversation with Zachary Flagg. They walked a little further and then the dog came running back, shaking water from its coat, with Jimmy in hot pursuit.

'You'll be careful, won't you?' Lucy said.

Mitchum looked down at her; their eyes met and held the other's gaze for a moment longer than was necessary.

'I will now,' Mitchum said.

Mitchum would have liked to get started early the next morning but he was expected to have breakfast and didn't want to let Lucy down. He had to admit it was well worth the delay. He had transferred his horse to a field adjoining Lucy's garden and his gear to a shed at the bottom of the garden which also served as a stable. As he was saddling up, Dr Robertson appeared.

'Lucy tells me you've not been following instructions,' he said.

'Shoulder's fine,' Mitchum answered.

The doctor took a look and changed the dressing.

'Seems OK but you won't do it any favours ridin' the range.'

When he had gone Mitchum eased into the leather and, turning away from town, splashed his horse across the stream. When he was on the opposite side he heard a shout and turned to see Jimmy waving at him from the garden. The dog was frisking about beside him. Mitchum waved in return. A lot of things seemed to be conspiring to hold him back so it hardly came as a surprise when he saw the figure of Flagg coming towards him down a turn in the trail. This time he was riding a horse rather than his mule.

'Figured you'd be earlier,' he said, riding alongside. 'I was waitin' at the livery stables. Woulda missed you if I hadn't taken a look out the back.'

'What are you doin' here?' Mitchum said.

'Showin' you the way to the cabin, of course. How did you expect to find it without me along?' There was the suggestion of an accusation in his piping voice.

'Didn't want to put you to no inconvenience,' Mitchum replied.

He realized that there was no point in trying to put the oldster off. It seemed he was stuck with him. At least it would make it easier to locate the shack.

The oldster at first was garrulous but as they rode further he became quieter. They settled to the rhythm of the ride, letting the horses go at their own pace. Unconsciously, Mitchum allowed Flagg to take the initiative: he was the one who was familiar with the country, he was the one who knew the best way to the shack. Later in the morning Mitchum heard what he thought was the distant whistle of a train but the trail they were following was unfamiliar to him. They seemed to be approaching the hills from a different direction. When they were well into the hills they stopped to rest the horses and grab a bite to eat. They drank water from their flasks and then mounted up again. The trail grew steeper and narrower. Then it levelled off and continued that way, alternating between steep and more level stretches, climbing from bench to bench with several turns and switchbacks. At one point, in a small valley, Mitchum saw some wild horses.

'Most of 'em are deeper in the hills and out towards the west where the country gets rougher,' Flagg said. 'They like to keep themselves to themselves.'

It was good country. For some reason Mitchum found himself thinking about Lucy. Had she seen much of it? His thoughts were interrupted when Flagg turned off the trail where it intersected with an even narrower one which led gradually downwards towards a grove of cottonwood trees. The trees looked nearer than they were and it seemed to take a long time to get anywhere near them. The horses were having to be careful, picking their way uneasily down the rough trail. It seemed clear to Mitchum that it was a track nobody used till he saw horse droppings. Easing from the saddle, he took a closer look.

'Not more than a couple of days old,' he said.

He looked about him. The sign was a little way off the trail and when he walked on he found further evidence of someone having passed that way. He pointed to a shoulder of the mountain.

'Looks like whoever it was came from that direction,' he said to Flagg. 'Is there a trail in from there?'

'Yeah. I don't suppose too many people are familiar with it.'

Maybe Mulligan had just been lucky finding the cabin, Mitchum reflected. Maybe there was something else to it. The evidence of the sign indicated that there had been more than one horse-man.

They mounted up and rode on through the trees. There was a stream at the bottom and Mitchum was about to cross when Flagg stopped him.

'We follow the stream,' he said. 'A little way along we leave our horses. The rest of the way we go on foot.'

It was darker among the trees. When they had gone about a further two miles Flagg indicated that it was time to dismount. Just ahead a tiny rivulet joined the stream.

'The cabin is further along that brook,' Flagg said.

They tethered their horses and crept forward. The diminution of the light was not just because of the tree cover; it was late in the afternoon. Flagg took a roundabout route through some trees so that they came on the cabin from the side. It stood in a little clearing with the rivulet trickling over stones nearby. One look at the place warned Mitchum that something was wrong. The door hung open and the ground in front was considerably scuffed. As they rounded the corner of the building, they could see traces of blood on the grass and spattered on the wall.

'You wait here,' Mitchum told Flagg. 'I'll go on and investigate.'

He crept forward, his Colt in his

hand. When he reached the open door he swung inside, keeping low and ready to fire, but there was no response. At an open window a curtain fluttered. As his eyes grew used to the dimness, he saw that the packed earth floor was stained with blood. The room was almost devoid of furniture: at the back an empty doorframe led into a second room. Padding carefully across the floor, Mitchum slipped though the doorway. At first he could see nothing but then he perceived something dark lying on the floor: the prostrate form of a man. Mitchum crept forward, expecting the man to be dead. Just as he was about to kneel down beside it, the figure gave a very low groan. If Mitchum hadn't been right beside the man, he wouldn't have heard. The figure was lying on its side. Carefully Mitchum rolled it over and then gasped. It was Marshal Stevens! Quickly recovering his composure, he put his ear next to the marshal's mouth. He was still breathing. Mitchum got to his feet and ran to the door.

'Flagg,' he yelled. 'Marshal Stevens is in here and he's been hurt. Get my flask from the Appaloosa and get back here quick!'

He ran back inside and after a few minutes the oldster re-appeared carrying the flask. It contained whiskey and Mitchum held it to the marshal's lips. As he did so the marshal's eyes flickered open and he murmured Mitchum's name. He swallowed a few drops and the glimmerings of a smile appeared on his lips.

'Sure glad to see you, Mitchum,' he whispered.

He became aware of another presence in the room and lifting his head slightly, he saw the figure of Flagg.

'Flagg? What are you doin' here?'

'Never mind that,' Mitchum said. 'How bad are you hurt?'

By way of answer the marshal pulled himself up to a sitting position.

'I'll be OK. It ain't the first time I bin buffaloed.'

Mitchum looked more closely at the marshal's head. There was a huge swelling at the back and his hair was matted with congealed blood. A thin trickle still ran down to his neck. It was a nasty wound but it did not seem to account for the amount of blood Mitchum had seen outside and on the floor of the cabin.

'Did you see who done it?' he asked.

'Nope. Somebody snuck up and poleaxed me from behind. I heard a shot. Then I guess I musta just passed out.'

Stevens's words about a shot probably explained the blood outside. But who could have fired it?

Darkness was rapidly falling and they decided to stay in the cabin for the night. They soon had a fire going in the grate and Mitchum laid strips of bacon in the pan. When they had eaten and had coffee boiling in a pot, they built smokes.

'How are you feelin' now?' Mitchum asked the marshal.

'Head hurts but this coffee hits the spot.'

Mitchum had given a brief explanation of their presence on the hillside but he wasn't clear about what the marshal was doing there.

'Doin' my job,' he replied. 'There's been two murders and someone took a pot at you.'

'Like I said, we figure it was Turkey Joe Mulligan,' Flagg said.

'Got an old dodger on him,' the marshal replied. 'When we get back, you can take a look to confirm whether or not it was Turkey Joe you saw.'

'It was Turkey Joe all right. I ain't one to forget a face.'

'I knew about this place. I just put two and two together. Looks like we were both right.'

There was quiet broken only by the drone of cicadas.

'The question now is; where we do go from here?' Mitchum said.

'What have we got?' the marshal asked.

'If you agree with us that the Quarter Circle Bucket had nothin' to do with those killin's,' Mitchum replied, 'then the situation seems to be that Turkey Joe was responsible. He's come after me and Hayes because of a grudge he bears for us puttin' him behind bars in the Red Rock days.'

'You say he's after you and Hayes. So why did he kill Darcy?'

Mitchum shrugged.

'Darcy was ridin' with Hayes. There were two of them. Maybe he had no choice.'

The marshal laid his head back and breathed out a couple of smoke rings.

'I'm thinkin' about that Wanted poster I got on Mulligan,' he said. 'Wasn't there more to that whole business? I seem to recall there was a big reward on his head for a train robbery. Didn't he get away with a lot of money? Nobody could pin that one on him. He stayed loose till you and Hayes put him behind bars for a wounding in Red Rock. Guess he must have been let out now.'

'Yeah, you've got it about right,' Mitchum said.

He stood up and walked to the broken door. The night was warm and they were grateful for the air which came in through it.

'Me and Hayes,' he mused, 'we were once on the trail of that loot Mulligan took from the overland express. Mulligan was a member of a gang called the Black Valley Forge boys because the first robbery that could definitely be pinned on 'em was near a place of that name. Turkey Joe was just another hoodlum in those days. It was only later he gained his reputation.'

There was a pause. Both the marshal and Flagg were listening closely, wondering what he was leading up to.

'I figure we got pretty close to locatin' that horde. The Black Valley Forge gang was broken up. The leader was killed tryin' to escape the law. He was the only one knew for certain where the loot was stashed. While we were ridin' up here I got a chance to think. I figure that Mulligan is not here just to gain revenge for us puttin' him in jail. I figure he thinks I got a pretty good idea where the loot is and he wants me out of the way in case I get there before he does. Maybe he's even under the illusion I know where it is.'

'Why would he worry? You ain't made any effort to find the loot in the time he's been in jail.'

'Varmints like Mulligan don't think that way,' Mitchum replied. 'They're too full of themselves to figure somebody might have other concerns.'

'You're right there,' the marshal interposed. 'I reckon there's a lot we could do to lessen crime if we studied the criminal mentality.'

'If I'm right, maybe he's tryin' to unnerve me. Remember, there's no reason for him to suspect that I know it was him killed Hayes.'

Mitchum returned to his place by the fire.

'Somethin' else I bin thinkin',' he said.

'Yeah, what's that?'

'While I'm in Sagegrease, people around me ain't gonna be safe. I can't stick around and put Lucy Wetherall and Jimmy in danger.'

'Ain't you exaggeratin' some?' Flagg said.

'Maybe. But even if it's only a faint possibility, it's a risk I don't intend takin'. Marshal, tomorrow you and Flagg ride back to Sagegrease and tell Lucy I had to leave.'

'She ain't gonna be happy,' the marshal said. 'Neither is little Jimmy. I figure that boy took a shine to you straight off.'

'It can't be helped. Don't tell 'em what's happened, just make up some sort of story.'

'That arm o' yourn ain't fully better yet.'

'It's a bit stiff, that's all. It ain't my gun arm.'

'And while we're attendin' to all this,

what are you gonna be doin'?'

'I'll be lookin' for Mulligan. He's left plenty sign. I'll catch up with him.'

'And while you're lookin' for him, he's gonna be lookin' for you,' the marshal said. 'If what you've said makes any sense.'

Mitchum nodded.

'Guess you're right,' he said.

What he didn't mention was the fact that he had seen sign of more than one rider. Who else was involved? Could Mulligan have teamed up with other members of the once feared Black Valley Forge gang?

Flagg poured himself another mug of black coffee.

'I ain't sure just how much sense this all makes,' he said, 'but I'll be happy to go along with it except for one thing.'

'Yeah? What's that?'

'I don't go back to Sagegrease with the marshal. Instead, I ride out with you, Mitchum, lookin' for Turkey Joe.'

Mitchum thought for a moment.

'I don't think that's a good idea,' he said.

'I ain't just proposin' to come along for the ride,' Flagg said. 'I might be getting a bit hoary, but I can ride, track and shoot as well as the next man. Besides, I been gettin' bored hangin' about the same old places.'

Mitchum shook his head.

'This is my problem,' he said.

'No it ain't just your problem,' the oldster replied.

'What do you mean?' the marshal said.

'When that train got blown apart by Turkey Joe, my brother got badly injured. He was one of the train guards. So you see, I got a stake in this too.'

Mitchum and the marshal looked at each other in shocked surprise.

'OK,' Mitchum said after a few moments, 'You're in. But first we both got to get the marshal back to Sagegrease.'

'That won't be necessary,' Stevens said, 'but I'd be grateful if you can just find my hoss.'

3

There was no problem following the trail left by Mulligan and whomever else had been at the cabin; the only trouble lay in finding a way up the steep trail that led away from the rivulet and up along the hillside. Eventually Mitchum and Flagg had to get down and lead their horses. It was hard going but as the top of the hill came in sight the ascent began to ease and they were able to remount. They came out just below the crest of the hill and the tracks were even clearer.

'What do you think?' Mitchum inquired of the oldster. 'How many of 'em?'

'Just two,' Flagg replied.

They rode on to where a rough trail intersected the one they were following and when they looked at the sign again it was obvious that the two riders they were tracking had been joined by two more.

'Seems like Turkey Joe has friends,' Flagg remarked.

Mitchum didn't want to keep anything from the oldster.

'I'm thinkin' that maybe some of the remainin' Black Valley Forge gang just got back together,' he said.

He hesitated for a moment, not sure how Flagg would take his next words.

'When you agreed to ride with me it was one against one. Now it's two against four. I'd understand if you decided to pull out and head on back to Sagegrease.'

Flagg grinned.

'I saw there was more than one person involved before we even got to the shack,' he said. 'I can read sign as well as you. Two against four is still pretty good odds.'

Mitchum smiled and nodded. He was getting to like the oldster better by the mile.

* * *

Marshal Stevens at that moment was sitting at the desk of his office in Red River. Ignoring Dr Robertson's orders, he had insisted on getting straight back to his duties. With a stiff drink near to hand, he was rifling through his drawers in search of a couple of old Wanted posters. A small pile of them littered the floor and one poster lay on his desk; Turkey Joe's face scowled from the page. Eventually he found what he was looking for and with a sigh of satisfaction he spread them out in front of him. In order to make sure of his facts, he had paid a visit to the undertaker where the corpses of the two gunmen Mitchum had shot were laid out. There was no mistaking the faces on the Wanted posters: they were the same men and both were former members of the Black Valley Forge gang.

He finished his drink, got up from his chair and stood for some moments by the window. The street outside was bathed in sunlight. People were going about their business; things were quiet since the Apple Bar outfit had departed for the Gulf. He reached up for his hat which was hanging on a peg, opened the door and set off down the street, walking towards the Wetherall house. Lucy was in the garden but there was no sign of Jimmy or the dog.

'They've gone down to the river,' Lucy said, 'with Jimmy's friend.'

'It's you I wanted to see,' he replied.

She raised her eyebrows.

'It's nothin' really,' he added.

He looked towards the house. The windows were open and a lace curtain fluttered from upstairs.

'If you're lookin' to see if Mr Challoner is around, he rode off again this morning.'

'Did he say where he was goin'?'

'No, but I imagine he is concluding his business with the Quarter Circle Bucket. Is that what you wanted to see me about?'

'Yes, but it ain't about anythin' in particular. It's just that, with the way things have been recently . . . '

'You mean the shootings?' she said.

'Yes, that and some other things. I just figured it might be as well to keep a closer look on who's comin' and who's goin' around town.'

'Really, Marshal Stevens, you're beginning to get me quite worried.'

The marshal feigned a laugh.

'Now don't you go and start worryin' none,' he said. 'There ain't no cause for that. I was wonderin', though, if you know anythin' about Mr Challoner?'

'Only what he's told me. That he's a drummer representing some firm that are in the Glidden wire trade. I know nothing about Glidden wire but whatever it is, Mr Bucket seems to have an interest.'

'And that's all?'

'I don't go poking into people's lives, Marshal. If I did, I could never run a boarding house like this. I take people as I find them. It's done me fine so far.'

'Sure,' the marshal said. 'I guess I'm just bein' over officious.'

He got to his feet and took his leave. As he walked towards the opposite end of town the smell of cattle grew heavy on the easterly breeze. The stockyards were built a little way out of town and he could hear the cows bellowing in their pens. He made his way to the railroad depot and stepped inside the shed. The man who acted as ticket collector, guard, and general dogsbody, Ed Mitchell, was sweeping the floor.

'Howdy, Marshal,' he said.

'Howdy Ed. I wonder if you could answer a question for me. A man called Challoner arrived in town recently. He's stayin' at Mrs Wetherall's at the moment. Can you tell me exactly when he arrived and where he came from?'

'Sure thing. We don't get so much traffic that I wouldn't remember him. He came in five days ago from Topeka. If you like, I could even find you his ticket stub.'

'That's OK,' the marshal said.

Stevens walked away towards the broad main street of town. As he went he was thinking: Topeka. Wasn't that near where the Black Valley Forge gang once operated?

* * *

At first it had been easy to follow the sign left by Turkey Joe and the other riders, but after two days on the trail Mitchum and Flagg had to admit that it had gone cold. Maybe an Indian would have been able to trace it. The country was high with long rolling hills and valleys. Mitchum placed his field glasses to his eyes, searching for anything which could indicate in which direction Mulligan might have gone. As far as he could see the land was empty.

'We should have been able to follow their trail,' Flagg said. 'Seems to me they took deliberate steps to try and conceal it.'

'Yeah. I was thinkin' the same. They must have an idea we are followin' 'em.'

'One of those boys was carryin' a wound,' Flagg said. 'That makes it even more likely they took steps to cover their tracks.'

'I got a theory on that,' Mitchum replied. 'I couldn't work out who could have shot him. It certainly wasn't the marshal. I figure the man was wounded before he ever got to the cabin. In fact, that was probably another reason the gang were headed that way. They were probably going to rendezvous with Mulligan. They figured the cabin would be a good place to tend to his injury. Instead of Mulligan, they found the marshal.'

'That still don't explain how he got shot.'

'No. But it means there could be somebody else lookin' for Mulligan and the Black Valley Forge gunnies apart from us. And he wasn't there for no reunion.'

'If we're right, then they know we're behind them. They could have us covered right now.'

'They could be leadin' us straight into a trap. Like the marshal said, they're lookin' for us just as much as we're lookin' for them.'

Mitchum looked through the glasses again.

'Do you know this country?' he asked.

'Some.'

'There's got to be a reason Mulligan is headed this way.'

The oldster thought for a moment or two.

'It's a long ways to go,' he said, 'but Red Rock is in this direction.'

'What, you figure he's aimin' for Red Rock?'

'That's where you nailed him. Maybe he's got some kinda warped sense that that's where he wants to return the compliment.'

Mitchum's brows were creased.

'You could be right,' he said, 'but I got a better idea. Between here and Red Rock is the Moccasin Range.'

'Yeah, I know it. Ain't but hills but it's pretty wild country.'

'It's where the Black Valley Forge

gang used to hang out. It's also where I figure they stashed the loot from that train robbery.'

The oldster gathered a ball of phlegm in his mouth and spat it into the dust.

'Not sure I catch your drift. Are you sayin' Turkey Joe is headed back to his old haunts? In that case, why would he have followed you to Sagegrease?'

'Because he wanted revenge. We know that. Only thing is, he figures I know more than I do about that missin' hoard.'

'Well, it all seems mighty speculative. But it's all we got to go by. We've lost Mulligan's trail. So why not head for the Moccasins? Maybe the air up there will be good for my health.'

Flagg spat again.

'Leastways, if you're right, Turkey Joe ain't likely to want you dead, at least for a while.'

'That's comfortin',' Mitchum replied.

As if to refute Flagg's statement, a shot suddenly rang out.

'Ride!' Mitchum shouted.

They dug their spurs into their horses' flanks and set off at a gallop, both men lying low. A burst of gunfire followed them; Mitchum felt a crump of air and his hat went flying from his head. He glanced back and saw a stab of flame from high on a hillside. They continued riding until the sound of gunfire dwindled in the distance and Mitchum reckoned they were out of range. Pulling his horse to a stop, he leaped from the saddle and ran part of the way up the slope of a hill. He put his glasses to his eyes again, sweeping the hillsides in the direction they had just come from.

'See anythin'?' Flagg shouted.

'Nope, not a thing.'

He walked back down the hill.

'What do you think?' Flagg said. 'Was that a botched dry-gulchin', or were they just givin' you another warnin'?'

Mitchum's mouth was set in a grim line.

'I don't know,' he replied. 'But I'm sure gettin' tired of bein' a sittin' duck.'

'One thing we know,' Flagg replied. 'We're on the right track and they ain't far ahead of us.'

'Yeah. And it seems like they want us to know they're still around.'

'They done a good job of coverin' their tracks,' Flagg said.

'Seems like a contradiction, don't it?'

'Whatever they're up to, they seem mighty confident.'

Mitchum climbed into leather.

'I wonder just how many of them there are now?' he said. 'And how many might be already waitin' up ahead in the Moccasins.'

* * *

Turkey Joe Mulligan was beginning to enjoy himself. It felt real good to be back in the swing of things, especially after those years in the Penitentiary. He was back on the owlhoot trail and with the Black Valley Forge gang reconstituted, he was truly on his way. He had revenged himself on Hayes and now he had Mitchum dangling on a string. To add to the fun, he had Cherokee George on board. Cherokee George knew all the skills of tracking and all the ways of concealing his own tracks. Cherokee was a volatile mix: part Anglo, part Cherokee with an admixture of Sioux and Mexican. He needed watching, but there was nobody better at doing what he did. There was no way Mitchum would catch up with him and when it came to locating that loot, Cherokee George's uncanny rapport with the terrain would be invaluable. Right now the group of them were gathered about the camp-fire. They had no fear of being detected by Mitchum or anyone else for that matter. Even Turkey Joe knew where and how to build a fire so it would not betray its presence. He was smoking a cheroot and in his hand was a bottle of Forty-Rod. He offered it to Cherokee George, who shook his head.

'So what you got planned for our friend Mitchum?' he said.

'I told you twice already.'

'Tell me again. Sure like to hear about it.'

Cherokee George turned his head to face Mulligan directly.

'What you got against this *hombre*? You sure seem to relish the prospect of drawin' it all out.'

Mulligan's expression changed.

'I spent three years in the Pen because of Mitchum,' he said. 'Besides that, he tried to destroy the Black Valley Forge outfit. He deserves to suffer before he dies.'

The quarter breed grinned, showing teeth that were chiselled to sharp points.

'That is the way to take revenge,' he said. 'It should be savoured. If you like, I will tell you of other methods.'

'Just tell me again about this one,' Mulligan said.

Across the flames, the other members of the group craned their necks to listen to Cherokee George's words, but this time they were to be disappointed.

'Enough. You talk too much,' Cherokee said. 'I have had plenty for one day.
I will see you in the morning.'

He stood up and walked to the back
of the clearing away from the fire.
Stretching himself on the bare rocky
ground, he closed his eyes.

'That *hombre* is sure one mean
coyote,' one of the men said.

'Yes,' Mulligan answered, 'but he is a
good dog to have around. And look
what he did for Patterson.'

The man referred to sat up. Across
his waist was wrapped a poultice.

'I don't know what he used apart
from the salt pork,' the man said, 'but it
sure seems to be doin' some good.'

He made to sit up and winced.

'Still hurts some,' he said. 'I'd like to
know who it was shot me.'

'You asked for it,' Mulligan replied.

He took another swig from the
bottle.

'It'll have to do till we can get you to
a doc,' he added.

'Cherokee George may be a coyote,'

another man said. 'But he's sure a wily one.'

Mulligan got to his feet and, walking a little way off, looked across at the wide vista of hills and valleys tinted to a silvery sheen by the light of the moon. Just in case anyone might see it, he stamped the glowing stub of his cheroot under his foot. Yes, it was good to be on the trail again. Things were going real well and if they continued that way, the loot from the railroad robbery would soon be his. And in the process, eventually, it would be goodnight to John Mitchum.

* * *

Marshal Stevens rode into the yard of the Quarter Circle Bucket and swung down from his horse. He tied the steeldust to the hitching rack and knocked on the ranch house door. Nobody answered but after a few moments one of the hands appeared.

'If you're lookin' for Mr Bucket, he's

gone down to the north range to take a look at some fencin'.'

Stevens got back into the saddle and headed for the north range. Before he arrived he saw three figures standing together and, nearby, a pile of timbers and a coil of wire. A wagon was standing nearby with some sort of equipment in it. As he got closer he could see that the three men were Bucket, his foreman Walt Grainger, and Challoner. He cursed under his breath. The presence of the drummer made things a bit awkward. They all looked up at his approach.

'Howdy, Marshal,' Bucket remarked.

'Howdy,' the marshal replied.

'You know Mr Grainger,' Bucket continued, 'but I don't know if you've had the pleasure of meeting Mr Challoner.'

When Stevens had dismounted, he tipped his hat to Grainger and shook hands with Challoner. He had been expecting something limp and weak and he was surprised by the firmnesss of Challoner's grip.

'Mr Challoner represents a business dealing in something called Glidden wire,' Bucket said. 'It's something quite new.'

Challoner took his cue.

'Maybe you're not familiar,' he said. 'It's a relatively new invention but it promises to revolutionize the way things are done.'

He bent down and picked up a piece of wire.

'This is a normal piece of wire. I guess you've used something similar plenty of times.'

He picked up another piece.

'Notice the difference,' he said.

Mitchum already had; he had pricked his finger on one of the barbs.

'Ordinary wire isn't cattleproof. This beauty was invented by a man called Glidden from my own state of Illinois. Those little sharp burrs sure manage to dissuade the critters from runnin' off.'

'Yeah, I guess they might. But wouldn't the cows get hurt? Any open cut would mean screw worm trouble.'

'Just what I said,' Bucket intervened.

'The cows soon learn. They get to respect the barbs, same way they respect natural thorns.'

Mitchum looked from one to the other of the three men.

'Seems like it's the way things is goin',' Grainger commented. 'Never took much to fencin' myself.'

'My friend,' Challoner said, 'you are right. It is the way things are going. The days of free range are drawing to an end. The Texas legislature already tried to ban the new wire but the bill failed. My advice to any rancher would be to start stocking up on the Glidden wire because soon there's not gonna be enough to go round.'

Bucket turned to the marshal.

'I been considerin' fencin' in at least part of the range. Too many horses break down the ordinary wire and get loose. I'm considerin' expandin' and goin' back into the cattle business. I got an advantage over those Texas outfits now that the railroad is so close.'

He paused and then laughed.

'Jumpin' Jehosaphat, we got so involved talkin' about this Glidden wire business I forgot to ask what you're doin' out here.'

Stevens glanced at Challoner but there was nothing to be read in that gentleman's features.

'It weren't nothin' much,' the marshal replied. 'Just thought I'd let you know there's no follow-up to that matter we were discussin' the other day. Seems like that little fracas had nothin' to do with any of your boys. Thought you'd like to know they're in the clear.'

'Don't worry me none,' Bucket replied. 'I knowed they weren't involved.'

He turned to his foreman.

'Still, it might be an idea for the boys to keep away from town, just for a while.'

'Sure thing, Mr Bucket.'

Stevens looked once more towards the drummer but he showed no interest in the turn the conversation had taken and the next moment he was doing something with the wagon. When he turned back again Bucket's next words were directed at him.

'You make a pretty good case,' he said. 'Just leave it with me for a few days. I'll give the matter a final few thoughts and discuss it with Mr Grainger. If you were to come back, say, in another couple of days, I could give you a definite answer.'

'That will be fine, Mr Bucket. I'll ride out the day after tomorrow.'

'I think the answer will be yes,' Bucket said encouragingly. 'I'm sure you'll appreciate, though, there's just a few matters need clarifying. Not as regards the wire; more with my plans for the ranch.'

'That's fine,' Challoner replied.

The marshal climbed back into the saddle.

'Are you sure that's all?' Bucket said. 'It's a long way to come for something so unimportant.'

'No problem,' the marshal said. 'Felt

I owed it to you.'

'Well, I appreciate it,' Bucket replied.

He turned to Challoner.

'Everything OK with Mrs Wetherall?' he ventured.

'I'm very comfortable. She's a fine woman.'

The marshal nodded and then, touching his spurs to the steeldust's flanks, rode away. Everything seemed above board with regard to Challoner and his intentions with regard to the Quarter Circle Bucket. Then why was it he still felt a slight unease?

★ ★ ★

It was the hour before dawn; Mitchum and Flagg lay asleep, rolled in their blankets. Flagg had suggested they take turns at keeping watch but Mitchum felt sure of his ability to wake quickly if anything untoward should present itself. He felt confident that Turkey Joe would not attempt anything by night. He might be a bushwhacker but creeping up on someone in the dark was not his line. He hadn't been in a position to take the presence of Cherokee George into the equation for the simple reason he was unaware that Cherokee George was riding with the Black Valley Forge gang.

At that very moment Cherokee George was watching the sleepers from the nearby bushes and calculating his final approach. The last embers of the fire had flickered out but the campsite was bathed in moonlight. He could not afford to take any chances. In his hand he held a box. When he was satisfied that Mitchum and Flagg were truly asleep and had mapped his final approach in his mind, he slithered forward into the open like the shadow of a snake. He crawled forward on his belly, making not the slightest sound, pressed flat to the earth so that even if either Mitchum or Flagg woke up, they would not see him. When he reached the edge of the burnt-out camp-fire he paused, moved slightly sideways and continued his silent approach. Slowly, slowly he inched his way forward until at last he was alongside the slumbering form of his victim. He could hear the slow regular susurration of the man's breathing. Gently he lifted the edge of the blanket and with infinite care undid the lid of the box he was carrying. A slight shake and something fell out, crawling its way beneath the blanket. For a moment Cherokee George's sharpened teeth glinted in the moon-light as he allowed himself a slight grin, and then he began to slither away, moving with the silence of a ghost into the shelter of some rocks at the back of the clearing. Only then did he raise himself as far as his knees and with a last backward glance over the moonlit glade, he disappeared into the night.

The first rays of dawn were just showing over the eastern hilltops when Flagg awoke with a start. He felt a stab of pain in his thigh and reached down. He felt something crawling down his leg and sat up with a start, striking at his trousers. His movement aroused Mitchum, who leaped to his feet, his Colt in his hand.

'What the — ?' he began but a howl from Flagg cut him short.

'I've been bit,' Flagg shouted.

Next moment he had leaped from his blankets and was tugging at his combinations.

'Scorpion!' he shouted.

Something fell to the ground and the next moment Flagg was pounding it with the heel of one of his boots. There was a sound like something brittle snapping but Flagg continued stomping till Mitchum took his arm and pulled him aside.

'Musta crawled in somehow,' the oldster yelled.

Mitchum knelt down and examined the partly mangled object.

'Afraid you're right,' he said. 'It's a scorpion.'

The insect was almost six inches long, its tail taking up half of its length.

'Hell, it hurts!' Flagg hissed.

He fell to the ground, clutching his thigh. The scorpion had got below the tail of his shirt and then inside his pants. Mitchum moved quickly to his tethered horse and got a canteen of water. Removing his bandanna, he began to wash the area of the bite.

'I hope you know what you're doin',' Flagg said. His face was wreathed in pain and a few beads of sweat had appeared on his brow.

'Just shut up and let me get on with it,' Mitchum returned.

When he had bathed the bite a few times, he soaked his bandanna in water and held it to Flagg's leg.

'Give me your neckerchief,' he snapped.

The oldster untied his bandanna with trembling fingers. Mitchum took it and wrapped it tightly round the compress he had made. He lifted Flagg's leg, elevating it as high as was comfortable.

'Hold it in that position,' he said.

The oldster groaned.

'You'll survive,' Mitchum assured

him. 'It's gonna be painful but scorpion bites aren't usually fatal.'

The oldster summoned a faded grin.

'That sure makes me feel a whole lot better,' he murmured.

Mitchum undid the bandanna to take a look at the wound. Flagg's leg was red and swollen. Soaking his own bandanna once more, he pressed it firmly down on the oldster's thigh again.

'How are you feelin' now?' he asked.

'Not so good. The leg feels like it's on fire and my tongue feels kinda swollen.'

'Let me take a look.'

Flagg opened his mouth and put out his tongue.

'Looks OK,' Mitchum concluded.

'My mouth feels kinda prickly,' Flagg said.

'That ain't the scorpion. That's just the way you are.'

Mitchum got to his feet and fetched his whiskey flask.

'Here, take a slug of this. It might help.'

The oldster took the flask and put it

to his lips. When he had drunk some of the whiskey he groaned aloud once more.

'How long is this likely to last?'

Mitchum had started to rebuild the fire. He looked across at Flagg.

'Not more than two, three days,' he said. 'Most likely less.'

When he had the fire going he made breakfast but Flagg was not up to eating anything. He decided that the best thing would be to give the oldster time to recuperate. Through the morning Flagg kept taking swigs of whiskey from Mitchum's flask, and by the afternoon he was sufficiently affected not to seem to mind the pain in his thigh.

'Let me take another look,' Mitchum said. The wound seemed quite a lot less swollen. 'Reckon you could stay on that horse?' he asked.

Flagg struggled painfully to his feet. 'Help me git on board,' he said.

Mitchum hoisted him into the saddle. The oldster's face was lined with pain and he didn't look too good.

'You sure about this?' Mitchum said.

The oldster nodded.

'Let's get out of here,' he said.

While he had been waiting for Flagg to recover, Mitchum had taken a good look round the area in which they had set up camp. At a couple of places he thought he saw evidence that the grass had been flattened but he couldn't be certain of it and in any case the impression might have been made by himself or Flagg. One thing he kept his eyes open for was any sign of scorpions. It didn't seem the kind of terrain to find them and he certainly saw no other indications of their presence. He looked at the insect's remains but he didn't know enough about them to be able to say where it might have come from. It seemed that Flagg had just been very unfortunate to find one among his blankets. Still, it was puzzling. He didn't say anything about it to Flagg as they rode away from the clearing.

* * *

When Marshal Stevens got back to Sagegrease it was late in the evening. There were still a few people on the streets and a number of horses were gathered at the hitch rail of the saloon. A fine night was in prospect. He picked up his favourite cane-bottomed chair and carried it out on to the boardwalk. The town was quite proud of its boardwalks; not many towns of a similar size and population could boast the same. He set the chair up where he had a good view of the street and stretched out his legs. He needed to think. His mind was vaguely troubled but he could not place a finger on what it was. It had something to do with Challoner. He went back over the conversation he had had with Challoner and Bucket that afternoon. There didn't seem to be anything odd about it; Challoner seemed to know what he was talking about and he had no reason to doubt that Challoner was anything other than what he claimed to be. So what was it? Why did he have a feeling that there was something slightly out of kilter about the discussion he had taken part in? Maybe it wasn't so much Challoner as Bucket. He began to stroke his chin. Bucket was old and had been retired for a long time. He had made his pile and the ranch was more of his plaything than a genuine working concern. So why would he be interested in fencing part of it off with Glidden wire? How had he even come to hear of it? His thoughts switched to Challoner again. If Glidden wire was the new thing and likely to revolutionize the business of ranching, why would Challoner be trying to sell it to Bucket? Wouldn't the natural thing be for him to concentrate his efforts on the big ranches down in Texas? Bucket didn't even run any cattle. He had said something about developing a herd, but even at the time it hadn't carried much conviction. So was something else going on? Was the Glidden wire a façade? If so, to cover what? And who was pulling the strings, Challoner or Bucket?

Rousing himself from his thoughts, the marshal began to look about him. Lights were coming on in some of the buildings. His eyes travelled the length of the street, lingering on the familiar store fronts and on the names: Green's grocery store, Madson's saddle shop, Westover's millinery, Jonson's livery, the barber shop, the clothing store, the bank. Then there was the Alhambra hotel, the Legal Tender saloon, Ross's eating house, and the other civic buildings; the Fire House, the bank, the schoolhouse, the newspaper office and printing press, the churches. Sagegrease had existed in embryo before the arrival of the railroad really put it on the map. It was a good place, but would it go the way of so many other cow-towns? What would it take for it to survive? Getting to his feet, he replaced the chair in his office before stepping down from the boardwalk and beginning to stroll down the main street. A cool breeze hazed a few clouds across the sky. As he walked his brain was still active. Had Challoner mentioned the name of the company he was working for? He couldn't remember Challoner saying it. Maybe it would be an idea to find out what it was and then see if there was some way of checking it. But where was the necessity to do so?

4

The next morning, Marshal Stevens paid another visit to Lucy Wetherall. He had a feeling that the drummer would not be there and he wasn't mistaken. Lucy brewed some coffee and then they sat together. Jimmy wasn't feeling so good that morning and was in his room. Rusty, the dog, stretched full length beside the marshal, looking up at him from time to time through plaintive eyes.

'I reckon you must make the best coffee in Sagegrease,' the marshal complimented Lucy.

'You sure you wouldn't like something with it?' she replied.

'No, thanks. This is just fine.'

He looked around the room. It was cosy, unlike his own front room in the house he rented from Normanston, the town lawyer.

'There was one thing I wanted to ask,' he said.

'Don't tell me it's about our friend Mr Challoner.'

'As a matter of fact, it is.'

'You seem to be taking an unusual interest in him.'

'Not really. I saw him yesterday out at the Quarter Circle Bucket. He seems to have made a convert of old Bucket to his Glidden wire.'

He paused and drank some more coffee.

'Well,' Lucy asked after a few moments, 'what was it you were going to ask?'

'I'm sorry,' Stevens replied. 'Plumb forgot what I was sayin' there for a moment. I just wondered whether Mr Challoner ever mentioned to you the name of the company he works for?'

Lucy murmured something, thought for a moment, and then shook her head.

'You know, I don't think he ever did mention it.'

'Has he talked to you about what he does?'

Again Lucy shook her head.

'No, at least not in any detail. Obviously he mentioned his occupation when he first came.'

'Can you remember what he said?'

Lucy was looking at the marshal with a questioning expression on her face.

'What's this all about?' she asked.

'Probably nothin',' the marshal replied. Quickly, he gave a brief account of his concerns about the drummer.

'I think you're making a fuss about nothing,' she replied. 'But, to go back to your question, all I can recall of our initial conversation was that Mr Challoner said he had some business at the Quarter Circle Bucket which was why he had come to Sagegrease.'

The marshal's attention was suddenly caught.

'He mentioned the Quarter Circle specifically?' he asked.

'Yes. Apparently Mr Bucket was interested in the Glidden wire. Is there something unusual about that?'

The marshal was trying to gather his thoughts.

'Maybe not,' he said. 'But then, how did he know about the Quarter Circle Bucket? It's unlikely Bucket would have been in contact with him. As far as I could see, Bucket knew nothing about this Glidden wire.'

'I think you are just being over suspicious,' Lucy replied. 'I can't see anything in it.'

The marshal got to his feet and took his leave.

'If Challoner says anything else that might be of interest to a suspicious mind, perhaps you could let me know?'

Lucy laughed.

'I certainly will,' she replied.

The marshal backed out of the door.

'By the way,' he said. 'Where is our Mr Challoner this morning?'

Lucy shrugged.

'He said he might not always be able to keep regular hours,' she replied. 'I imagine his business requires him to stay over with a client from time to time.'

'Yeah, that's quite likely.'

As he walked away down the street, the marshal was reflecting that Challoner had told Bucket he would be back in a few days. He had given no indication then that he might be staying over.

*   *   *

Flagg had suffered a setback in his recovery from the scorpion bite. That night he felt quite ill and it was the same the following morning. There was nothing to be done except wait for the poison to work its way out of his system. Mitchum sat up most of the night keeping watch over the sick man, but knowing that there was little help he could offer other than to be there. Shortly before dawn the oldster fell into a fitful slumber. Towards the evening of the second day though, he began to perk up and it was clear that the worst was over.

'Sure could do with somethin' to eat,' he said.

Mitchum grinned.

'How are you feelin' now?' he asked. 'Apart from bein' hungry.'

'Feel like I bin bit by a scorpion but it's OK now. Must be about breakfast time.'

Mitchum explained to him that most of another day had gone by.

'Hell,' the oldster replied. 'We'd best get movin' or that varmint Mulligan will get clean away.'

'Just what I was thinkin',' Mitchum replied. 'I figure we should push on towards those Moccasins and travel by night. But not until we've both got a plate of ham and beans and a pot of coffee inside us first.'

By the time he had eaten and enjoyed the strong black coffee, Flagg was feeling pretty well restored. The moon had swum up over the hills and the sky was full of stars.

'Let's get goin',' the oldster said. 'I'm

just about ready for anythin'.'

They climbed into leather and set off. Their path led over the brow of a hill and then around the shoulder of a rocky outcrop. The panorama of hills stretching ahead of them was breathtaking in the glimmering moonlight.

'Man, that sure is pretty,' Flagg said.

Away in the distance some taller peaks could be just discerned rising above the intervening hills.

'Those must be the start of the Moccasins,' Mitchum said. 'But they're further away than they look.'

They rode on, the trail now leading downwards into a wooded coulee. On one side the cliff face was steep and cast the coulee into deep shadow. Away on the other side they could hear the trickle of running water. Looking up, Mitchum could see a pattern of caves and ledges high on the hillside. Then he saw something else. The face of the mountain seemed to be moving, silently and as if in slow motion. He blinked his eyes, thinking it was some effect of the moonlight shining on the side of the hill. He remembered once, when he was a boy, seeing the stars falling down the sky and being scared by the enormity of it until his senses adjusted and he realized it was not the stars tumbling but the scudding clouds. For an instant that image from the past played itself out again and then his ears discerned a low rumbling sound and he was jerked back to reality.

'Rockslide!' he shouted.

The sound was deafening now and the horses reared in fright. In a moment they were back under control as Mitchum and Flagg began riding hard down the track in a desperate race to get ahead of the falling boulders. A huge stone hurtled through the air just head of them, causing the horses to veer, but they kept on going. Large stones and small were bounding and leaping down the hillside, blocking the path they had just ridden. Some of them launched themselves further to go crashing into the streambed. The light of the stars was concealed behind a cloud of dust. They rode on at a frantic pace, the roar of the landslide fading behind them, till the noise gradually dwindled to a trickling and shifting as the smaller rocks and stones continued to fall and settle. Mitchum glanced over his shoulder. The danger seemed to be past and they drew their quivering steeds to a halt. In the gloom they could see that the path was now blocked. If they hadn't reacted quickly, they would have been buried beneath the rockfall.

'That was a close thing!' Flagg commented.

Mitchum's eyes were scanning the hillside above.

'Guess we were unlucky the landslide started just when it did,' Flagg said. 'Or plumb lucky to outride it.'

Mitchum continued to scrutinize the hill but it was too dark to make anything out.

'I don't reckon that was an accident,' he said.

'Not an accident? What do you

mean? What else could it have been?'

'I reckon that Turkey Joe Mulligan is up to his tricks again,' Mitchum said.

The oldster let Mitchum's words sink in.

'But if that were Turkey Joe's doin', he must be watchin' us.'

'That's about the size of it,' Mitchum remarked. 'We figured he'd be well ahead of us by now. That's what he figured we'd think. He's playin' games with us.'

The oldster was quiet for a moment before speaking.

'Mitchum.'

'Yeah?'

'If you're right, then what do you make of that scorpion?'

Mitchum looked hard at the oldster.

'What do you think?' he said. 'I reckon that scorpion bein' in your blanket was no accident either.'

The oldster looked aghast.

'And what's more,' Mitchum continued, 'I reckon it was probably meant for me.'

The oldster scratched his chin; it made a slight rasping sound in the darkness.

'Well,' he concluded. 'No offence, but I sure hope they pick the right man next time.'

Mitchum took a last long look at the hillside.

'There's plenty of places they could hide,' he said.

'Maybe we'd best get ridin,' Flagg replied. 'I don't know about you but I'm beginnin' to get a mite uncomfortable knowin' they're up there.'

'I wish we had a better idea just how many,' Mitchum said. 'Could be some of 'em have rode on ahead while others have remained behind to keep us tagged.'

'All we can do is head for those Moccasins,' Flagg replied. 'See what happens then.'

'Guess you're right.'

They set off down the trail.

★ ★ ★

Marshal Stevens was sitting in Ross's eating house, drinking coffee and wondering how Mitchum and Flagg were getting on. He had not given the pair of them a lot of thought since the day they had set off in pursuit of Turkey Joe. Now his reflections had taken a new turn. Mitchum had arrived in Sagegrease with the Apple Bar outfit. At that time the marshal had found it a little curious that the former marshal of Red Rock would be taking part in a cattle drive. Casting his mind back, he remembered that Mitchum had said he had done it to oblige his friend Hayes. So was it just circumstance that brought them both to Sagegrease at the same time as the mysterious drummer? And how had Turkey Joe known about it? There were too many coincidences. However, it might begin to make more sense if Hayes' involvement with the cattle drive had not been accidental. What if Hayes had had a purpose in choosing to travel all the way to Sagegrease? What was Challoner really doing at the Quarter Circle Bucket?

His thoughts turned to the ranch. It covered a lot of land but Bucket didn't seem to do much with it. The ranch house itself was large and elaborate and unlike anything he had ever seen before. And what about all those works of art, fancy furnishings and expensive wines and spirits? Bucket had a lot of his things imported from back east and from overseas. The Quarter Circle Bucket was an expensive hobby. Where did all the money come from? Then he recalled Mitchum's comments about the Black Valley Forge gang and the railroad robbery. There was yet another coincidence. He looked out of the window at the broad, dusty street, as if he expected to see Challoner. The drummer had not returned to town after visiting the Quarter Circle Bucket. Was he still somewhere out there? The marshal sprang to his feet. There was only one way to find out. And this time he would not be letting Bucket know anything about it.

When Marshal Stevens arrived at the Quarter Circle Bucket, it was late at night. Cloud had driven up from the south and the land was dark. When he reached the boundary line, he turned off the trail leading to the ranch house. He didn't know what he was looking for but all his senses were alert for anything unusual which might help focus his scattered thoughts and suspicions. His eyes flickered here and there and he felt strangely nervous. As he continued riding a thin chill rain began to fall, making it difficult to discern anything. On the other hand, it made it difficult for anyone to see him. He rode more slowly, scanning the rain-driven landscape. It seemed a long time before he perceived a dark smudge against the dreary background. He couldn't make out what it was at first but as he got closer he could see that it was an old line cabin with a lean-to building that probably served as a stable. There was nothing unusual in that and yet something made him pull his horse to a

111

halt. He peered hard at the ramshackle building, his face contorted into a scowl. Then he heard the faint stamp of a horse's hoof. He glanced behind him, his first reaction being that some rider was creeping up on him. Then he realized that the sound had come from within the lean-to stable. He swung down from the saddle and began to inch his way towards the line cabin.

When he reached it he flattened himself against the wall, listening intently. The rain continued to fall, spattering on the sod roof of the building. He heard a shuffling of hoofs from within the lean-to and began to move back to see if he could take a look inside. The ground was getting soggy and as he stepped back his boot slipped and he staggered sideward. At the same moment the door of the cabin flung open; there was a stab of flame and the report of a rifle as a bullet went flying past his shoulder. If it wasn't for the slip, he would have taken the bullet full on. In a moment his six-gun was in his hand and he returned fire. A second bullet crashed into the wall beside him. It was impossible to see anything. Crouched low, he ran to the corner of the stable and slipped behind it, thinking to double-back and catch his assailant in the rear. Inside the lean-to stable, the horse began to whinny. He came round the building when suddenly there was a flash of lightning and for a brief moment the looming shape of a man was outlined against the sky. In that moment he thought he recognized who it was.

'Challoner!' he called.

Thunder rumbled overhead.

'Challoner! It's Marshal Stevens!'

The thunder crashed down the sky. Stevens had pressed back against the cabin and dropped to one knee, seeking to make himself invisible. His eyes searched for the other man but he couldn't see him. Then a voice called to him out of the whispering darkness.

'Stevens. What the hell are you doin' here?'

'Never mind that!' Stevens called back. 'You almost killed me!'

'I didn't know it was you, Stevens. I just figured whoever it was meant trouble.'

There was a moment's pause.

'Listen, this is gettin' silly. I'm getting' plumb wet too. I'm puttin' my gun back in its holster and steppin' clear.'

Stevens hesitated for just a second. He realized he was taking a slight chance. He stood erect and walked away from the shadow of the cabin.

'I see you, Stevens. I'm doin' the same.'

A little way ahead of Stevens the darkness of the night gathered to a thicker shade. Both men moved forward until they could see each other properly.

'Step inside,' Challoner said. 'It ain't much but it's better than bein' out here in the rain.'

When they were inside Challoner lit a kerosene lamp.

'Make yourself comfortable,' he said.

Stevens glanced round the shack. There were two chairs, a rough deal table and a mattress. On a shelf stood a few tins of food and a half-full bottle of whiskey. The only note of comfort was a low fire flickering on the grate. Stevens pulled up a chair and Challoner did the same.

'Sorry about the shootin',' Challoner began. 'There's no way I could have known it was you.'

Stevens pulled his tobacco pouch out of his pocket, picked out some tobacco and a paper, and passed the pouch to Challoner. They both lit up.

'I'd say you were still a mite quick on the draw,' Stevens said.

'Yeah, maybe so. But I had a right to do so. Besides, hangin' out here gets a man kinda jumpy.'

'Just what's goin' on?' Stevens said.

Challoner made himself more comfortable and took a long drag on the cigarette before replying.

'How much do you know?' he asked.

'Nothin,' Stevens replied. 'I'm workin' on the killing of Darcy and Hayes. You've met Mitchum? Hayes was Mitchum's friend, leastways used to be. Someone called Mulligan took a shot at Mitchum. I don't know how or where you fit in.'

'What are you doin' here? What made you suspect me?'

'Like I say, I'm pretty much in the dark there. One thing I reckon I'm right about, and that is you ain't no drummer sellin' Glidden wire for a livin'.'

Challoner let out a low chuckle.

'And I thought my alias was real good. Thought I had everybody fooled.'

'You did with most everyone else. Almost had me fooled.'

'I did a lot of work studyin' up on that wire thing.'

'So who are you? And what are you doin' in Sagegrease?'

Challoner looked into the spluttering flames of the fire.

'Guess you'll have to know the truth,' he replied. 'You're an officer of the law.

We're on the same side. But I assume I can rely on your complete discretion about what I'm goin' to say.'

'Of course,' Stevens replied.

'Challoner is my real name, Gus Challoner, but I ain't no drummer. I'm a Pinkerton agent. If you like, I got the papers to prove it.'

The marshal looked across at the other man.

'Yeah,' he said, 'I think I'm beginnin' to see it now.'

'You ask what I'm doin' in Sagegrease. You may know something about a robbery which took place some time ago involving, among others, the man you just named, Joe Mulligan, known as Turkey Joe.'

'Yeah. In fact I was takin' a look at some Wanted dodgers recently related to the incident.'

'The robbery was committed by a group calling themselves the Black Valley Forge gang. A lot of money was taken. None of it has been recovered — yet. To cut a long story short, I've been on the trail of the money for a long time and I have reason to believe that there is a connection to our friend Mr Bucket right here on the Quarter Circle.'

Stevens sat up straight.

'Of course!' he snapped.

Challoner glanced at him with a look of surprise on his face.

'Sorry, just goin' back to some recent thoughts of my own.'

'A man would need to have an awful lot of cash to buy and maintain the Quarter Circle Bucket.'

'Especially when he does nothin' with it,' Stevens intervened.

'Precisely. My investigations have convinced me that Bucket was involved indirectly in that train robbery. The law had nothin' on him, however. It's my theory he got away with a good share of the loot and used it to buy the Quarter Circle.'

'You say a good share. You mean he didn't get away with all of it?'

'I'm almost certain there's still a lot

of it stashed away someplace. Bucket probably knows where. It could even be right here on the Quarter Circle. It's a long shot but wherever it is, I mean to locate it.'

Stevens got to his feet.

'Care for a drink?' he asked.

Challoner nodded and Stevens poured whiskey into a couple of cracked glasses. When they had taken a swallow Stevens returned to the subject of the missing loot.

'Seems like Turkey Joe Mulligan and some of the old Black Valley Forge gang are on the trail of that cash,' he said.

'Yeah. In fact I'm certain of it. I had to shoot one of 'em.'

'At a cabin in the hills?' Stevens asked.

'You know about that? I tracked Turkey Joe up there but almost got taken by surprise by some of his cronies.'

'Mitchum and Hayes put Turkey Joe behind bars. He's out for revenge. That's why Hayes got shot.'

Challoner took another swallow of the whiskey.

'Where's Mitchum now?' he asked.

'Tryin' to track Turkey Joe. Either that or bein' tracked by Turkey Joe.'

Challoner looked askance but didn't make any remark.

'So you figured to hole up a while in this cabin while you take a good look around for that loot?' Stevens resumed.

'That's about the size of it. Looks to me like no one ever uses the place now. No reason for anybody to stay out here; ain't no cattle to keep an eye on. I figured the money might possibly be hidden somewhere hereabouts. Could be worse places to keep it concealed.'

'Found anythin'?'

Challoner shook his head.

'Nope. I guess that would be too much to expect.'

Mitchum flicked the stub of his cigarette into the fire.

'Are you sure no one knows you're here?' he said. 'You're takin' a bit of a risk with that fire.'

'Ain't seen no one.'

'Not even durin' the day?'

'It's a big spread. As far as I can tell, Bucket keeps a token workforce. There ain't a lot of work to be done. I tried to sell him on the idea of keepin' a few head of cattle.'

'That Glidden wire story is gonna run pretty thin,' Stevens said. 'I'm surprised Bucket gave it the time of day.'

'Yeah, that thought had struck me too. I'm beginnin' to wonder whether Bucket ain't got his own suspicions.'

'In which case, things could get pretty hot for you,' the marshal said.

'I have to meet with him again day after tomorrow. I was hopin' for some sort of breakthrough before then.'

'If you're right about him, he's probably been checkin' on you,' Stevens said. 'I was thinkin' of doin' the same myself.'

The fire had burned low while they were talking. Outside, the storm had abated: although lightning still flickered, the intermittent boom of thunder was fading.

'Reckon we'd better check on those horses,' Challoner said.

Stevens had brought his own horse into the shelter of the lean-to and both men got to their feet and moved to the door. When they opened it they stood for a few moments before Challoner turned to the marshal.

'Do you hear somethin'?' he said.

Stevens nodded.

'Riders,' he said. 'Looks like Bucket has got wise to one of us.'

Without waiting for further confirmation, they moved quickly to the outhouse and saddled up the horses. Stevens climbed into leather.

'Hold it just a moment,' Challoner said.

He disappeared back inside the cabin and reappeared with his rifle.

'OK,' he said, placing his foot in the stirrup. 'I think it's about time we got out of here.'

They set off at a gallop, keen to put

some ground between themselves and Bucket's men. After a time they stopped to listen once more and they could hear the unmistakable sound of hoofbeats. They rode on again at a steadier pace. Presently from a long way behind them they saw a blaze of light.

'Looks like they've set fire to the cabin,' Stevens said.

The glow of the flames spread and they could see showers of sparks flying in the air.

'I guess you could say it's been a mighty eventful night,' Challoner replied.

'Let's hope you were right about that loot not bein' stashed in the cabin,' Stevens said. 'If so, looks like Bucket just burned it.'

They watched for a little while longer till the flames began to subside.

'Where to?' Challoner said.

'Back to Sagegrease, I guess. You'd better not walk in on Lucy Wetherall. Guess you'll have to stay at my place for the time bein'.'

Stevens paused to consider.

'Then day after tomorrow we both ride on back. It'll be interestin' to see Bucket's reaction to all this. Lookin' at what happened to that cabin, I'd say your alibi just got mighty shaky.'

'Yeah. It's gonna take some brass neck to carry on with that drummer routine.'

'Give it a final go. We'll see what happens.'

Touching their spurs to their horses' flanks, they rode on.

★   ★   ★

Mitchum and Flagg had been riding blind, unable to pick up the trail of Mulligan and the others, but knowing that if they kept on going, Mulligan would be tracking them. As they approached the lower slopes of the Moccasins Mitchum detected sign.

'Two horses,' he said. 'Question is, is it some more of the Black Valley Forge gang or someone else?'

124

'Don't seem likely that there'd be other riders up here,' Flagg replied.

The sign seemed to indicate that the riders had come from a different direction to the one they had been following.

'Judgin' by the way they're headed, they could be aimin' for Red Rock,' Mitchum said.

He paused before adding: 'Maybe it's time we split up.'

The oldster scratched his chin.

'Now just why do you figure that?' he said.

'Because Mulligan won't be expectin' it.'

'So what you got in mind for me?'

Mitchum continued to weigh up the situation.

'I figure you should follow this sign. If I'm right, it'll take you to Red Rock.'

'What then?'

Mitchum shrugged.

'I don't know. That's why you should go. See if you can pick up anythin'.'

The oldster glanced about him.

'And what about you? Are you carryin' on into the Moccasins?'

'Yeah. I got a hunch about that lost loot and I want to follow it up.'

'How long's that gonna take you?'

'I ain't sure. Could depend on what Mulligan has in mind. Let's give it a couple of days. That'll give us both time. I'll see you in Dutch Pete's saloon at sundown in two day's time.'

'Dutch Pete? You figure I'll find the place all right? You ain't been in Red Rock for a while.'

'Don't worry, you'll find it,' Mitchum laughed.

'Sounds like I'm gettin' the best of this arrangement. Wouldn't say no to a night or two between the sheets.'

'Just be careful whose sheets they are,' Mitchum said.

Flagg regarded him with a look which was suddenly serious.

'Make sure you're there at Dutch Pete's,' he said. 'Don't forget that Mulligan might be foolin' about some but in the end he's out to get you.'

Mitchum's eyes were cold steel.

'I ain't likely to forget that,' he said.

The two of them shook hands and then stepped into leather. Neither of them looked back as they rode off in their separate directions. Michum was wondering whether Mulligan had been observing the scene. Whether he was or not, events were drawing to some sort of climax and that was one more reason why he had wanted the oldster out of the way. Whatever Flagg had said, Mitchum still considered it was his affair. Now that a confrontation with the Black Valley Forge gang was imminent, he owed it to the oldster to consider his safety. It was a slim chance that the sign he had detected had anything to do with the Black Valley Forge gang. Instinctively reaching for his rifle, he set his course for the higher ranges.

5

It was the evening of the day and little Jimmy was about ready to go back to his house.

'Rusty, hello Rusty,' he called.

He looked about him. The late sun glinted from the waters of the stream which at this point ran shallow over flat stones that glistened dark brown beneath the surface. In places long streamers of green weed rippled back like strands of hair. Dragonflies flew among the rushes and willow trees leaned over the water. On the opposite side the bank was flat and the meadow ran down to the stream in a long slope.

'Rusty, come on boy!'

Jimmy looked left and right. There was an answering bark and the dog burst into sight, running towards him. At the same time Jimmy became aware of two riders who came slowly down the slope on the other side and splashed their horses into the stream. The bank on which Jimmy stood was steeper and their horses had to make a bigger effort to step out of the water. Jimmy turned away from the riders and began to run towards the dog. Before they met he became aware of a clatter of hoofs. A dark shadow overhung him and a hand grabbed him by the collar of his shirt. He stumbled another pace before being hoisted into the air. For a moment he hung there and then he was dropped to earth again as the dog leaped and sank its teeth into the rider's boot. The man cursed and his horse reared. Jimmy began to run. A shot rang out behind him and Jimmy stopped, fearing for the dog more than himself. Tears were blinding his eye but to his relief he saw the dog chasing after him and yelping. The rider Rusty had attacked was still struggling to get his horse under control. Jimmy turned and started to run again, shouting loudly for help. In another moment his house hove into view and then the figure of his mother appeared. He shouted louder and waved his arms as she came towards him. The dog was running at his side and soon he was in his mother's arms. Still sobbing, he raised his head from her skirts and looked back. The two riders were fast disappearing, riding hard along the river bank.

'What is it? What happened?' his mother said.

He tried to explain but his tears and sobs rendered him incoherent.

'Quickly, let's get you inside,' Lucy said.

She looked down at the dog. Blood was oozing from its side. Bending down, she picked Jimmy up and walked as quickly as she could to the garden gate and up the path to the house. She sat the boy on a chair.

'Wait for just a moment,' she said.

She went to the back porch and looked along the river bank but the riders had gone. She became aware that she was shaking. She returned to Jimmy who for the first time realized that the dog had been hurt. His concern for the dog seemed to calm him down.

'Rusty's injured,' he said.

Lucy bent down and examined the dog. As far as she could see, the wound was superficial and Rusty certainly didn't seem to be too concerned. She went to the kitchen and returned with a wet rag.

'Tell me what happened,' she said as she bathed the dog's wound.

In broken sentences Jimmy explained what had occurred.

'It's all right now,' she said.

She was trying not to let the boy sense how upset she was. She glanced at the clock and found herself wishing that Mitchum was around, that he would soon come through the door. She realized how much she was missing him.

★　★　★

Mitchum was fully aware of the dangerous course he was pursuing, but he could see no other way out of the situation he found himself in. If he was ever to be in a position to deal with Mulligan and the rest of the Black Valley Forge gang, he first needed to flush them out into the open. Mulligan wanted two things: to get the information about the missing loot out of him and then to dispose of him. The only flaw was that Mitchum did not know where the loot was stashed. He had some notion but that was all. It would be no good trying to convince Mulligan of that fact. But there was no other solution. He had to walk into the trap deliberately and put himself at the mercy of Mulligan and his gunslicks. Once he was in their power, he would have to rely on luck and his own wits to save him. That was why he had encouraged Flagg to ride on to Red Rock.

As he rode he was aware that the outlaws probably had him in their sights. It made him feel uncomfortable. The only consolation was that while Mulligan was under the illusion that Mitchum knew where the railroad loot was hidden, it was unlikely that he would simply shoot him. Somewhere close by Mulligan and his men were concealed. Mitchum's eyes scanned the hillsides for any indication of their presence but he could see nothing suspicious. Mitchum was thinking that Mulligan and the rest of the Black Valley Forge gang were probably not sophisticated enough to be able to cover their tracks so well and remain undetected. That meant they had someone riding with them who had the necessary skills. He must be somebody who knew all the ways of making himself elusive; somebody who could creep up on a camp in the middle of the night undetected and slip a scorpion into a sleeper's blanket. Somebody with those sorts of credentials might have Indian blood in him. Suddenly he gave a little chuckle. He had an inkling who that person might be. Cherokee George. Was it possible? Stranger things had happened. If it was Cherokee George, his chances of survival were a lot better. He had known Cherokee a long time and had ridden with him on several occasions. It was Cherokee George who had acted as scout on a few missions behind enemy lines in the War between the States. Cherokee George. Already he was beginning to feel a lot more confident. Then almost immediately his mood changed. Even if he was right about Cherokee, what was he doing riding with Mulligan? Why had he dropped that scorpion into Flagg's blanket? Maybe Cherokee had changed — he had always been a volatile character. If so, if it was Cherokee and he was now on the wrong side of the law, Mitchum's fate might be worse than he imagined. Cherokee George knew some ways of slowly killing a man that would make even Turkey Joe blanch.

Mitchum continued riding. His plan was to carry on as far as the area where he figured the loot was probably stacked. Turkey Joe would either jump him before then or wait to see if Mitchum made any move to locate the money. Mitchum hadn't been up in the Moccasins for a long time and he was looking for any familiar landmarks. He couldn't see anything that he remembered. One location seemed pretty much like another. He was looking for a particular minor trail which led along the side of a hill that was pockmarked higher up by a number of caves. He skirted several hills, each of which might be the one he was looking for. On a slope a short distance away he saw a line of trees climbing a hillside which looked familiar. Behind it the serrated line of an edge sliced into the skyline. He brought the horse to a halt in a grassy meadow to take a closer look through his field glasses. That combination of serried trees and jagged backdrop seemed to be what he was

135

looking for and he could just make out the faint line of what seemed to be a trail heading round the shoulder of the hill. He put the field glasses away and rode on. It took longer than he had anticipated to reach the point where the side trail diverged to follow the line of the hill, but he felt reassured that he had found the right spot. He turned off and immediately the trail began to climb quite steeply. The land to his left fell away in a succession of hills and valleys, till it rose to form another range behind which he guessed was the trail leading down eventually to Red Rock. He thought about Flagg. How far had the oldster still to go? He would be a lot better off in Red Rock.

The trail he was following led through some trees before emerging again high on the side of the hill. Up there, a strong wind was blowing straight into his face, but as he continued the path took a wide turn and he found himself in the lee of the breeze. Across a wide valley the crest of the opposite escarpment bit like teeth into the azure sky. The going was easier now as the trail levelled off. He was halfway up the hill, looking for the caves which he remembered being between where he was and the summit. The horse was sure-footed and used to high country but there was no need for concern because he was riding along a wide grassy ledge and the slope on either side was gentle. Any lingering doubts about whether he had found the right trail were finally banished when, after riding a little further, he saw the dark outlines of caverns in the hillside up ahead of him. Narrow tracks led up to some of them and continued up the slope to the summit of the hill.

Stopping once more, he got out the field-glasses to take a closer look. The cave entrances were of varying sizes; the largest of them overhung ledges on some of which trees and bushes were growing. There was water up there. At the top of the hill the slope was steeper in places but nowhere was it so steep that a man couldn't climb or a horse make its way down. The hill culminated in a ridge which led along the top for a long way into the distance. Concentrating his attention on a couple of the wider tracks leading down from the summit, he observed that they seemed to be churned up more than would be accounted for by the natural effects of weather and he saw what looked like horse dung near the edge of the tracks. He put the glasses down. There could be only one explanation: Turkey Joe and his gang were there ahead of him, probably waiting for him in one of the caves or on the ridge above. Normally he would never have left himself as exposed as he was, but under the present unusual circumstances it didn't matter. In fact, it was what he wanted. Now he needed to go the rest of the way and ride straight into the trap. He touched his spurs to the horse's flanks and rode forward, his eyes flickering between the trail ahead and the caves on the hillside.

He was almost abreast of the first one but there was no sign of Turkey Joe. A glint of light made him turn in the saddle and he saw two riders skylined on the crest of the hill behind him. He turned his head the other way; coming up from the valley were two more riders. They must have been well concealed because he had seen nothing through the field glasses. He pretended to take no notice and rode slowly on. Above him was the entrance to a large cavern marked by a fall of stones which formed a low mound at one end. Emerging from the gloom of its interior a number of figures were materializing. They carried rifles and some of them were pointing at him. In the centre of the group which now numbered five he recognized Turkey Joe and next to him the unmistakable figure of Cherokee George. Mitchum hadn't seen either of them for a long time but, like Flagg, he didn't easily forget a face. His life might depend on it. He had a sudden doubt of the wisdom of his plan to deliberately spring the trap Turkey Joe had set but it was too late now for second thoughts. He became aware of an intense quiet which muffled the hills like a Navajo blanket. High above, a buzzard soared. The silence was suddenly shattered by a loud voice which went ringing across the valley.

'Mitchum! Nice of you to pay us a visit.'

Mitchum stopped the horse and looked up towards the cave.

'Ride right on up. We got a welcomin' committee just waitin' to make your acquaintance!'

Mitchum remained sitting his horse, saying nothing. Out of the corners of his eyes he was aware of the approach of the riders behind him. One of their horses whinnied. Mitchum's horse began to shake its head.

'What are you waitin' for, Mitchum? We got a lot of things to catch up on!'

Mitchum tugged on the reins and the horse began to slowly climb the narrow trail leading to the cave.

'Better leave your guns behind!' Mulligan yelled. 'Just drop 'em right there for the boys to collect.'

Mitchum stopped again, reached for his rifle and threw it to one side. He undid the buckle of his gun-belt and dropped his Colts to the grass. Then he rode on till he reached the level ground in front of the cave entrance. The outlaws' rifles were still pointed at his chest.

'This ain't right friendly,' Mitchum said. 'How about you get your boys to put away the artillery?'

Turkey Joe grinned.

'OK boys,' he said. 'Put 'em down. We don't want to scare our guest.'

A couple of the men chuckled and one of them spat. Mitchum's eyes were on Cherokee George. He alone appeared to be unarmed. His face was inscrutable and his eyes were blank. Mitchum slid from the saddle.

'Turkey Joe Mulligan,' he said. 'Last time I saw you, you were runnin' scared of the Blake boys. Guess you were almost glad I put you behind bars. I hear the Blake boys are still feelin' real sore about the way you let 'em down.'

Turkey Joe's grin changed instantly to a frown. Mitchum noticed the way a couple of the outlaws looked across at him.

'You'd better learn to keep your mouth shut,' Turkey Joe snapped.

'Sure. Wouldn't want to embarrass you in front of these fine folk,' Mitchum replied.

Turkey Joe stepped forward and with a muttered oath he brought the butt of his rifle crashing into Mitchum's stomach. Mitchum doubled up as Turkey Joe's rifle swung up and caught him on the chin. Blood spurted and Mitchum fell in a heap at Turkey Joe's feet.

'I told you to keep your mouth shut!' Turkey Joe hissed.

He turned to some of his men.

'Pick him up and bring him inside,' he ordered.

Mitchum felt himself being lifted

from the ground. His stomach hurt like hell and he thought he was going to retch. Blood was pouring from his chin which was cut to the bone. The light of day faded as he was half carried and half dragged into the twilit depths of the cave and then vanished altogether as he slipped into the soothing balm of unconsciousness.

* * *

Marshal Stevens was at his desk when the door to his office opened and Dr Robertson came in. He was looking agitated and annoyed.

'Got me a new patient,' he said.

Stevens glanced at him with a puzzled expression.

'A four-legged patient goes by the name of Rusty.'

He had the marshal's attention now.

'Yeah, that's right. Seems like the dog took a bullet in the side protectin' young Jimmy Wetherall from a couple of no-good varmints tried to kidnap him.'

'When did this happen?' Stevens said.

'Just yesterday. I'd like to get my hands on the scum.'

'How is Jimmy? And how is his mother?'

'They'll be fine. Surprised they ain't been in to see you.'

Stevens got to his feet and reached for his hat.

'I'd best get out there right now,' he said.

The doctor shook his head.

'Lucy's stayin' at my place,' he said. 'Wilmer wouldn't hear of them goin' back to their house.'

Stevens paused.

'You'd better tell me the whole story,' he said, sitting down again.

When the doctor had told him as much as he knew, Stevens was back on his feet.

'Did Lucy have any idea who might be responsible?'

'Nope. She wasn't there when it happened and little Jimmy wasn't able to say much.'

Stevens thought for a moment.

'I'll head down to the river,' he said. 'See if I can pick up any clues. What time will you be back?'

'Not till late. Wilmer will be there though if it's Lucy you want to see.'

The marshal stepped out of the door and climbed into leather. It didn't take him long to reach the riverbank where he had been told Jimmy was playing when the two men attacked him. It didn't take him long either to find the imprints of their horses. He could tell from the sign just where they had ridden up out of the stream and he crossed over to the other side, following their trail till it became confused with the tracks of other horses. The riders seemed to have come from the direction of the Quarter Circle Bucket. That did not mean very much in itself but it seemed significant when taken together with the fact that Challoner had been staying with Lucy Wetherall. Maybe it was a coincidence but Stevens didn't think so. It was another piece of the jigsaw. But if the riders were Bucket's men, why had they attempted to kidnap the boy? The whole episode meant that there was one more reason to approach Bucket with care when he and Challoner rode out to the Quarter Circle next day. Satisfied that there was nothing further to be found by the river, Stevens rode back to the doctor's house.

* * *

Mitchum came round to a throbbing pain in his head and jaw and when he attempted to move he winced as a further stab of pain shot through his stomach. He was in pitch darkness, lying on hard rock; as things began to come back to him he realized he was in the recesses of the cave. He figured he must be well back because no firelight reached him and, though he strained his ears, he could hear no voices. Bracing himself against the pain he knew must come, he struggled to sit up

146

again. This time he succeeded. His teeth were gritted and he took time to take some deep breaths. The air was surprisingly fresh and when he looked up he could see the faintest suggestion of light high on the cavern roof. There must be an opening up there. Gradually his eyes began to adjust to the darkness until he could dimly perceive his surroundings: rock walls with knobbly protuberances, uneven rock floor, and the immediate gloom receding into blackness and obscurity.

With a big effort he succeeded in getting to his feet. After waiting a few moments, he took a tentative few steps back. They were enough to tell him that he was almost at the rear of the cave. Turning round, he began very slowly to make his way forwards. He had to take extreme care because the place was so dark and he had a fear of stepping into some kind of void. Before each step, he felt in front of him to ensure that he was placing his foot down safely. In this manner he groped his way forward, his face clenched against the pain involved. At least he had no worries about banging his head; from what he had seen of the light source, the cave was high if not wide. He kept towards one wall and after a time it took a bend. As he progressed the darkness grew less palpable and it was obvious that he was moving towards the entrance. Presently he could see quite well and then, rounding another bend, he saw daylight ahead and knew he was approaching the mouth of the cave. So far he had seen no sign of anyone but as he staggered forward he could see the shape of a reclining figure with his back against the rock. For a moment he stopped but then tottered on again. He had no choice in the matter. The daylight grew brighter and he shielded his eyes. The man lying at the cave mouth turned his head; it was Cherokee George.

Mitchum reached the cave mouth and sank to the floor. Cherokee George observed him coldly.

'Guess you could maybe do with some water,' he said.

Mitchum nodded. Cherokee George reached behind him and handed Mitchum a canteen of water. Mitchum put it to his lips and the liquid revived him.

'You don't look so good,' Cherokee George commented.

Mitchum poured some of the water over his head and winced again as it ran over his wounded chin.

'Where are the rest of 'em?' he asked.

By way of reply, Cherokee pulled a tobacco pouch out of his pocket and handed it to Mitchum. There were papers inside and Mitchum built himself a smoke. He handed it back and Cherokee did the same. When he had taken a few pulls on the cigarette, he spat and directed his attention to Mitchum.

'Some of 'em are along there,' he said.

He nodded in the direction of another cave which Mitchum recognized as the one from which the outlaws had originally emerged.

'The others will be back soon.'

'Aren't they bein' a bit careless?' Mitchum said.

The shadow of a grin appeared on Cherokee's face.

'If you're referrin' to yourself,' he said, 'I'd say you were in no fit state to do anythin'.'

Mitchum leaned his back against the rock.

'They got plans for you,' Cherokee continued.

'Yeah? Maybe I got plans for them.'

Cherokee George emitted a low mirthless grunt.

'Like I said, I don't think you're in a condition to do much about it.'

There was silence for a few minutes. Mitchum was feeling a bit better but he had to admit Cherokee George was right. He looked along the ledge where the other caves were situated and caught a reflection. He looked up and saw a man with a rifle high on the hillside above them. His observations were interrupted by the voice of Cherokee.

'Yup, I'd say your case was just about hopeless. But who knows, maybe there could be a way.'

Mitchum turned his head.

'What do you mean?' he rapped.

'Well now. Seems to me you got just one bargainin' chip.'

'What's that?'

'Turkey Joe seems to think you know where that railroad stash is buried. That's the only reason you're still alive.'

'Turkey Joe is wrong,' Mitchum replied.

Cherokee spat again.

'Maybe he is and maybe he ain't. Me, I figure it's worth takin' a chance that you do. And if I were you, I wouldn't go denyin' it too long or too loud. Not if you want to keep on livin'.'

'So what are you sayin'?'

'I'm sayin' I'm willin' to take a chance that you know more than you're lettin' on. I'm sayin' that it makes a lot more sense to divide that loot between two than share it with Turkey Joe and his band of losers.'

Mitchum was thinking hard.

'You might be makin' sense if I knew where the money is,' he said.

'You got at least a better idea than anybody else.'

'Even if that were true, it still don't mean I'd be likely to find it.'

'Well, that's as maybe. Put it this way. Either you take a chance with Cherokee George or you let Turkey Joe and his boys beat the truth out of you.'

Mitchum took a long drag on his cigarette.

'Was it you put that scorpion in Flagg's blanket?'

'Flagg? That the name of the oldster you were ridin' with?'

'Yeah. He weren't too happy about it.'

'I doctored that scorpion,' Cherokee George replied. 'Best part of his sting got removed.'

'Coulda fooled Flagg,' Mitchum replied. 'It took him most of a couple of days to get over it.'

'That snake Mulligan must have substituted another one. Seems like he don't trust nobody. I figured he had me down as suspect all along.'

'Why do it at all?'

Cherokee George shrugged.

'To keep Turkey Joe sweet. Seems to me that man just ain't right in the head.'

Mitchum took a final drag and then stubbed out the fag end of his smoke.

'OK,' he said. 'Maybe I got an idea where to find that loot. So what do we do next?'

★ ★ ★

It was after midday when Stevens and Challoner arrived at the Quarter Circle Bucket. If Bucket knew of Challoner's real identity or simply had suspicions, he gave no indication of it. He was out on the veranda of his extravagant ranch house as they rode into the yard and gave every sign of welcoming their arrival.

'Come straight on in,' he said as they slid from the saddle. 'Hargreaves, take their horses and give 'em some feed.'

When they sat down he poured them drinks.

'Best Irish whiskey,' he said.

Stevens was casting his eye over the room without making it too obvious. He had been in the ranch house a number of times but now he looked at it with renewed interest. He didn't know what he hoped or expected to see but there was nothing to arouse his suspicions.

'Well, Mr Bucket,' Challoner began. 'Have you had a chance to consider the matter of the Glidden wire any further?'

Bucket twirled his glass.

'I've thought about it a great deal and had further discussions with my foreman, Mr Grainger. We both agree that your Glidden wire is just the thing if we're gonna fence in part of the upper range. Like I said, my concerns were not so much about the efficacy of your product as about the plans I have in mind for the ranch.'

'And if it's not rude to ask, what are those plans?'

'I'm thinking of investing in cattle. Now the railhead is right on our doorstep it would seem to make sense. I've been conducting negotiations with a view to buying a herd of some twelve hundred cattle and they'll need to be fenced off.'

Stevens started.

'That's a lot of cattle,' he said.

'At the moment they're selling at a good price. I've arranged to buy six hundred at six dollars a head and another six hundred at three dollars a head.'

Stevens was doing some quick calculations in his head.

'That's twelve hundred cattle at an average price of $4.50 per head.'

'That's about it. Put another way, that's forty cents a hundredweight. Gross.'

Stevens whistled silently.

'Of course, I'll need to add to the remuda. I can supplement it later by roundin' up some of those wild horses in the hills.'

'All that means more cowhands,' Stevens remarked.

'It's a big job and it don't end there. I have other plans which I need not bore you with.'

Bucket turned back to Challoner.

'I guess that means a good lot of wire,' he said.

Stevens was observing Challoner closely, wondering how the Pinkerton man would react to Bucket's interest in the Glidden wire. Would Challoner be sufficiently well versed in his role to carry the business to a realistic conclusion? Maybe Bucket's whole line was a sham. He thought the time was perhaps right to introduce a new element into the conversation.

'By the way, I thought you might be interested in somethin' which happened in town.'

'Yeah, what's that? Hope you ain't

accusin' my boys again.'

'Ain't accusin' anybody. Less'n you know somethin' might cast light on the matter.'

'What matter?'

'Seems like an attempt was made to kidnap little Jimmy Wetherall. Couple of *hombres* rode up and tried to snatch him. Luckily they didn't succeed, largely thanks to the intervention of Rusty.'

'Rusty?'

'His dog.'

Stevens had the impression that Bucket was slightly put out but he couldn't be sure.

'So what's that got to do with me?'

'Nothin' in particular. I'm tellin' a lot of folk. Who knows, somebody might know somethin'.'

'Why would anyone want to take a little boy?' Bucket asked.

'That's what I'm tryin' to find out. I'd appreciate any thoughts you might have on the matter.'

A look of something approaching

anger flickered for an instant over Bucket's features.

'How should I know!' he snapped.

'You know that Mr Challoner has been lodging with Lucy Wetherall during his stay in Sagegrease?'

'Then maybe he might be in a better position to throw some light on this kidnap affair than me,' Bucket retorted.

Challoner took up the challenge.

'Beats me,' he said. 'Can't figure it out. I haven't had much to do with the little fella time I been here. He sure seemed to take to Mitchum, though.'

Bucket turned to the marshal.

'Mitchum? Ain't he the *hombre* you brought with you when you were tryin' to accuse my boys of those two murders? Sounds to me like he's the man you should be talkin' to.'

'Don't worry. I will. Just as soon as he gets back.'

Stevens knew he had Bucket's attention.

'Gets back? Gets back from where?'

The marshal shrugged.

'I don't know. Seems he had to go chasin' after somebody. Can't just remember the name — somethin' kinda weird. I got it; someone he used to know called Turkey Joe Mulligan.'

There was no doubting now that Bucket was perturbed, although he tried not to show it.

'Strange name,' he said. 'Is he likely to be gone for long?'

'No idea. Whatever it's about, it's Mitchum's business, not mine.'

Bucket took a big large swig of his whiskey and rapidly poured himself another.

'Well,' he said, turning to Challoner. 'Looks like we got a little distracted. But as far as that Glidden wire is concerned, we got us a deal. Why don't we shake hands on it right now and we can go into the details later.'

'Sure. Anytime,' Challoner replied.

'I tell you what,' Bucket continued. 'I aim to pay a visit to town soon. Why don't I meet you in the Alhambra? If you have the papers ready, we can do some business.'

'Sounds good to me.'

'OK. Let's say tomorrow around noon. I'll stand you somethin' to eat.'

'Even better,' Challoner replied.

'You must excuse me right now, gentlemen. And thanks again for stoppin' by.'

Stevens and Challoner got to their feet. It was clear to both of them that Bucket wanted them gone. He accompanied them to the stable where their horses had been left. They mounted and rode slowly away. Bucket watched them leave and then began to walk quickly in the direction of the bunkhouse.

As they put distance between themselves and the Quarter Circle Bucket, Challoner turned to Stevens.

'I'd say that Bucket was a bit rattled about somethin' you said. I reckon he knows more about that kidnappin' affair than he's lettin' on.'

The marshal grinned.

'So it wasn't just me got that impression,' he replied.

'He was swallowin' a lot of that whiskey. And his handshake seemed a mite sweaty.'

The marshal's eyes instinctively observed the landscape they were riding through.

'I'll tell you somethin' else,' he said. 'He showed a lot of interest in Mitchum's doin's. I'd be almost prepared to believe that there's some connection between him and Turkey Joe Mulligan, even if you hadn't mentioned it.'

'He seems to have a lot of cash on hand,' Challoner remarked. 'That's a big investment he's proposin' to make in cows.'

'Yeah. Not to mention the Glidden wire.'

It was Challoner's turn to grin.

'I'd better be gettin' down to that paperwork,' he said.

6

Mitchum crouched behind a bush and watched as Cherokee George approached the guard he had seen on top of the hill.

'Howdy,' the man said.

'Howdy,' Cherokee George replied.

'Shouldn't you be watchin' that cave?'

The man's voice betrayed an element of surprise but he had no reason to feel suspicious about Cherokee George.

'I can't wait for Turkey Joe and the boys to get back,' he continued. 'Man, there's goin' to be some fun tonight when we get to work on that coyote Mitchum. By the time we've finished, he'll be pleadin' to let us know just where that loot's hidden.'

'Yeah. It's gonna be a lot of fun.'

The man glanced away, looking along the ridge that topped the hill. It was his last move. Mitchum saw Cherokee step forward and then the man fell to the ground. There was no sound and no indication of anything untoward having occurred. For a moment Mitchum thought the man might have stumbled but in a few moments the figure of Cherokee George, which had momentarily disappeared from his vision, appeared walking back towards him.

'We had better move quickly,' Cherokee said.

It required a real effort of will for Mitchum to act. The climb up the hill had exhausted him but he knew that he had no choice in the matter. Cherokee George led the way and Mitchum followed. Once they reached the crest of the hill Cherokee George signalled for Mitchum to lie down. Cherokee's eyes swept the ridge and looked over into the wide valley which lay on the other side, searching for any signs of movement. Mulligan and most of the other outlaws had ridden out to reconnoitre the stagecoach route which lay in the general direction of Red Rock. On the way they were looking out for Mitchum's partner but they weren't too bothered whether they found him or not. It was Mitchum they were after and they had him where they wanted.

When Cherokee was satisfied that there was no one in view on the other side of the ridge, he signalled to Mitchum. Still taking precautions not to let themselves be seen, they crossed the ridge and began the opposite descent. It was hard going for Mitchum and he was relieved when, about half-way down, Cherokee gave the signal to halt.

'I can't see anythin',' Mitchum said.

'That's why it's a good place to hide.'

Cherokee moved sideways to a clump of bushes. Pulling them aside, he revealed the narrow entrance to yet another cave. This one, though, was little more than a burrow and Mitchum had to crawl in order to gain access. The floor sloped down a little way and then the passage opened out before becoming impassable slightly further on. Mitchum surmised that the whole hillside was honeycombed with underground passages and caverns. It was something like this narrow tunnel which probably led down to the roof of the cavern in which he had awakened and seen the glimmer of light above.

'Ain't exactly homely,' Mitchum remarked.

'It'll do,' Cherokee said. 'We ain't gonna be stuck here for long. Once Turkey Joe gets back and finds we're gone, he'll assume you overcame me somehow, hid my body and made your escape.'

'How about that man on top of the hill?'

'All the better. They'll assume you did for him too. Pretty soon they'll be out searchin' the whole countryside for you. That's when we'll have our chance to double back and search that cave where you reckon the loot's hidden.'

'Like I said, it's only a hunch. What if I'm wrong and there's nothin' there?'

Cherokee's face was impassive in the gloom.

'You'd just better not be dealin' from the bottom of the pack,' he said.

Time passed. Cherokee cut strips of jerky and handed some to Mitchum.

'Guess you must be gettin' kinda hungry,' he said.

Mitchum hadn't been aware of hunger till Cherokee George mentioned it. Once his attention had been drawn to it he realized how hungry he was.

'How long was I lyin' in that cave?' he asked.

'A whiles.'

It was now early in the afternoon. Mitchum reckoned he must have slept or been unconscious for most of a night.

'You figure Mulligan is aimin' to rob the stage?' he asked.

Cherokee indicated his unconcern with a shrug of the shoulders.

'He seems to have got it into his head that the Black Valley Forge gang is back in business,' Mitchum mused.

There was no immediate reply from Cherokee. Presently he spoke again.

'That's a plumb strange kinda name. Where did they get that from?'

'Black Valley ain't too far from here. The gang used to operate in the area down as far as Red Rock.'

'That how you come across 'em? I can tell you, Turkey Joe still seems mighty sore about what happened.'

'Kind of,' Mitchum replied. 'I got him for somethin' else altogether. His days of ridin' with the Black Valley Forge gang were about over.'

Mitchum was almost thinking aloud.

'The place wasn't just a forge. There used to be an old tradin' station there. People used to stop by on their way through, originally mountain men and trappers. Later it became quite well known as a rendezvous.'

Suddenly he sat up, almost bumping his head against the ceiling.

'What's up with you?' Cherokee said.

'I just had an idea.'

'Musta been a good one.'

Mitchum turned to his companion.

'What if the loot is hidden at Black Valley Forge?' he said.

'Why should it be?'

'Hell, I don't know, but the more I think about it the more reasonable it seems. Why didn't I think of it before? The place would be ideal. The outlaws made a lot of use of it — it was right in the middle of their range of operations. The place is probably deserted now.'

'Wouldn't Turkey Joe have worked it out for himself?'

'Turkey Joe would probably think it was too obvious. He figures the loot is hidden some place up here, in one of those caves. Same as I did. Until now, that is.'

Cherokee was chewing on a strip of jerky.

'You ain't tryin' to trick me?' he said.

'No, I ain't tryin' anythin'. If you like, we can still take a look at that cave. If there's nothin' there, we could take a ride to Black Valley.'

Silence fell between them. Each man

was thinking his own thoughts. It was only broken when they heard the sounds of riders coming down the hill. There were quite a few of them and their voices could be heard.

'That'll be Turkey Joe,' Cherokee whispered.

The riders passed close by.

'They'll have split up,' Cherokee said. 'Some of 'em will be startin' down this side of the hill. They'll spread out lookin' for you.'

'How many of them are there altogether?' Mitchum said.

Cherokee reflected for a moment.

'About a dozen,' he said. 'Maybe a few more.'

They both listened for any further sounds. When they were satisfied that the coast was clear they made their way outside.

'What do we do?' Mitchum said.

'We take a look in that cave. Maybe you were right in the first place.'

Mitchum was getting back to his old self. The short climb across the brow of the hill and back to the caves left him short of breath and still aching, but he was beginning to feel a lot better. The outlaws appeared to have left nobody behind and they quickly made their way into the cavern that Mitchum had marked down as the likeliest spot for the loot to have been concealed. Sunlight was pouring into the entrance where some of the outlaws' belongings were scattered. A few saddles hung from hooks in the wall. The lantern which Cherokee George produced seemed superfluous until they had made their way towards the back of the cavern. The place was bare.

'Maybe there's some kind of ledge or hole in the wall.'

They looked closely up and down, examining the rock walls for any signs of hidden nooks or crannies.

'What about the other caves?' Cherokee asked at length.

'There's no point,' Mitchum replied. 'I reckon this whole hill is riddled with caves and passages. If they brought the loot up here, it could be hidden anywhere within it.'

'I guess they wouldn't have made it easy to find,' Cherokee replied.

They made their way back to the cave entrance. Cherokee George looked up at the sky.

'Sun's beginnin' to go down,' he said. 'Turkey Joe's likely to be back any time.'

He looked closely at Mitchum.

'You wouldn't be holdin' out on me?' he said.

'I want to find that money as much as you.'

'You're a lawman. You want that money so you can give it back again.'

'Ex-lawman,' Mitchum said. 'Look, you're right; I don't want any of that loot for myself. But there's a reward out for anybody who finds it. You'll cash in anyway.'

'I know about that reward. It's a lot less than takin' the whole stash.'

'You won't have to look over your shoulders for Turkey Joe or the rest of the Black Valley Forge boys.'

Cherokee laughed ominously.

'I got ways of dealin' with Turkey Joe,' he said.

Mitchum's ears picked up a sound from outside.

'You'd better have. I reckon Turkey Joe's back again.'

Cherokee didn't wait for further conversation.

'Come on,' he said. 'Grab one of those saddles and we'll take a couple of horses.'

They made their way along the ledge and began the climb to the top of the ridge where Cherokee signalled to Mitchum to crouch down. Riding up from the valley floor were a group of riders among whom Mitchum could pick out Turkey Joe.

'Keep low and stick close behind me,' Cherokee hissed.

He slithered forward, hesitating just a moment before hoisting himself level with the ridge. Mitchum followed and they edged forward on their stomachs till they reached the drop on the other side. They slipped over the rim and, standing up again, began to run in the opposite direction to where they had hidden in the tunnel, towards a grove of trees. Before they were half way there Mitchum could hear the stamp of horses' hoofs and when they came into the trees he could see a few horses tethered. One of them was his own horse. Wasting no time, they saddled up.

'I'm puttin' a lot of trust in you,' Cherokee said.

Mitchum looked at him without understanding what he meant.

'Here,' Cherokee said, 'take these. I expect you're gonna need them.'

Reaching behind his saddle, he produced an Allin-Springfield rapid fire rifle and a revolver.

'I keep the rifle handy although I don't make much use of it myself. Prefer the Sharps. Sorry about your own rifle and guns.'

Mitchum took the weapons. He tucked the revolver into the belt of his pants and hefted the rifle before placing it in the empty scabbard where his own rifle had been.

'Thanks,' he said.

'Just so long as you don't forget who the enemy is and point it at me,' Cherokee said.

Stepping into leather, they rode the horses through the trees, emerging lower down the hill at a spot where they were at least partly concealed from the heights. The slope was not steep but the going was still slow as the horses picked their way down. Just as the hillside was levelling off and they were believing that they had got away unnoticed, the peace of the hills was shattered by a rifle shot.

'Looks like they seen us,' Cherokee shouted. 'Let's move it!'

'Guess it weren't a good move to waste time lookin' about that cave!' Mitchum replied.

Further shots rang out from above them as they dug their spurs into their horses' flanks and set off at a gallop down the valley. Mitchum glanced up. There were four horsemen on top of the hill and as he looked they were joined by another. The horsemen began to descend the slope of the hill but he and Cherokee were already out of range of their bullets. Mitchum faced forward and relaxed. The outlaws had just returned from a hard ride and their horses would be tired. They had a good lead and there was little chance that they would be caught. They kept riding hard and when Mitchum looked back again the hill and the riders had receded into the distance. The only trouble was that they had been spotted at all. It meant that Turkey Joe and his gang would be on their trail and not far behind. And it wasn't so far to Black Valley Forge that they would be able to shake them off.

★   ★   ★

Stevens and Challoner sat at a table in the dining room of the Alhambra hotel.

A number of people sat at the surrounding tables but the place was relatively quiet. Things would be different, Stevens reflected, when the next trail outfit hit town. Above the low mumble of conversation he could hear the ticking of a large grandfather clock standing by the opposite wall. It said 12.35.

'Well,' he remarked. 'Looks like our friend Mr Bucket isn't goin' to turn up after all.'

Challoner looked out of the window at the prospect of the street.

'Can't say I'm particularly surprised,' he said.

Stevens nodded his head in agreement.

'Me neither.'

'Do you reckon he really intended payin' a visit to town like he said last time we spoke to him?'

'Maybe. But more likely it was an excuse. He certainly seemed to be uncomfortable when he mentioned it.'

The clock ticked on; the pendulum

swung. Before either could resume their conversation, a man sitting at the next table unexpectedly leaned forward.

'Excuse me,' he said, 'but I couldn't help overhearing the last part of your conversation. I gather you are waitin' for Mr Bucket.'

'That's right,' Stevens replied.

'In that case, I think you may be doomed to disappointment. I saw Mr Bucket and a group of his ranch-hands riding away from Sagegrease just yesterday.'

Stevens was suddenly interested.

'You know Mr Bucket?'

'Sure. He's the owner of the Quarter Circle.'

'And you're sure it was him?'

'Yeah, I'm sure. I was comin' in from the hills and they rode right by me.'

'Thanks,' Stevens said. 'Appreciate the information.'

The man turned back to his own table. Stevens and Challoner looked at one another.

'Now that's interestin',' Stevens said.

'I wonder what Bucket could be up to.'

'Whatever it is, looks like he needs to have some of his boys along.'

Stevens was thoughtful.

'Looks like they were headed towards the hills. And whatever Bucket's up to, it seems to be pretty urgent.'

He looked at the empty plates lying on the table.

'I'd say we were about finished here,' he said.

'Yeah,' Challoner replied.

They got up, walked from the room and kept on walking till they got to the livery stables. Neither of them felt the need to say anything more. Without wasting any time they saddled up and then rode out in the direction of the hills.

★ ★ ★

Stevens had been wrong about Bucket when he surmised that his statement about visiting town was an excuse. Bucket had indeed intended going into town about some business but events had conspired to make him change his plans. Things were moving too fast for his liking. He was almost certain that Challoner was not a travelling salesman but some representative of the law. Then the marshal seemed to be uncomfortably inquisitive. Finally he had learned that Turkey Joe was back on the scene. The comfortable illusion of ease and tranquillity he had built up since the time he had acquired the Quarter Circle had been broken. Now he needed to act quickly. Suddenly he felt old. What was he to do? What course of action should he follow? It would have helped if he had been more certain how matters stood. How much did any of them know about the hidden loot? He had intended replenishing his stocks anyway in order to pay for the changes he envisaged for the Quarter Circle. His plans to introduce a herd of cattle had been ripening for some time. He would have had to pay a visit to Black Valley Forge sometime, although it was not something he relished having to do. Now his hand was being forced. Since he could not be sure how general the knowledge about Black Valley Forge had become, it behoved him to be decisive and get there without any further delay. But he felt unsure and mistrustful of his own judgement. It hadn't been a very clever move to attempt the kidnap of the boy. He hadn't been thinking straight. Was he thinking straight now? It was all very confusing. In the past he had enjoyed the part of eminence grise. He was more suited to a role behind the scenes, manipulating the action and remaining shadowy and anonymous. It was how he had served the Black Valley Forge gang, providing them with funds and equipment, teasing out the information they needed to plan their operations, being the brains behind their activities. Now he was having to play an active role just at the time his powers were waning, when he had expected to carry on his self-indulgent life style without concern for the past. At least he could count on Grainger. He didn't ask questions as long as he was well rewarded. Although it was something he didn't want to have to do, he might have to rely on him more in the future. And the next step had to be to get to Black Valley Forge before anybody else figured exactly where that loot was hidden.

*   *   *

Cherokee George climbed up to the edge of the hollow where he and Mitchum had set up camp for the night and looked out across the darkened landscape. Turkey Joe and the Black Valley Forge gang were so close behind that he could see the faint glow of their camp-fire in the distance. He calculated that there were no more than five miles between them but it didn't worry him. He knew how to maintain that distance. He knew he could increase or decrease it as he wanted, depending on the circumstances. It would only be when the outlaws finally got up close that the odds would be all against them. That didn't really worry him either. He was stoical about the outcome and he knew enough about Mitchum to be comfortable about having him at his side when it came to the final roll of the dice.

Down in the hollow below him the flame of their own fire cast flickering shadows among the bushes. Mitchum was lying nearby, smoking a cigarette and nursing a tin mug of coffee in his hands. He was fully recovered from Mulligan's assault on him with the rifle but his chin was badly damaged. It was lucky that the jaw wasn't broken. Cherokee George slithered back over the lip of the hollow.

'Turkey Joe still there?' Mitchum said.

'Yeah. Right behind us.'

Cherokee poured himself a mug of coffee.

'How about we slow him up a bit?' he said.

Mitchum looked up and grinned.

'Now that sounds a real sensible idea,' he replied.

'We could hit him right now,' Cherokee replied. 'He won't be expectin' visitors.'

Mitchum tossed the stub of his cigarette into the fire.

'What are we waitin' for?' he said.

He poured the remains of the coffee over the fire and they strolled to where their horses were tethered. In a matter of moments they were on their way.

At first Mitchum could see nothing but after a little while he could see the faint glow of Mulligan's fire.

'Better not get too close,' Cherokee said. 'Don't want to skitter their horses.'

When they were sufficiently close they tethered their own horses and went forward on foot. The flickering glimmer of the outlaws' camp-fire was strange and unearthly. As they got close they expected to hear the occasional sound of a voice, even though the hour was late; the sound of a horse's snicker or the shuffle of a hoof. Cherokee paused and seemed to almost sniff the air.

'There is no one here,' he said.

'How can you be sure?'

By way of reply Cherokee crept forwards again, stopping in the cover of some vegetation which overlooked the campsite. As Mitchum came alongside he carefully parted the bushes.

'See!' he whispered.

The fire had burnt low but by its glow Mitchum could see that the place was deserted. Drawing his six-gun, he was about to step into the open when Cherokee held him back.

'Be careful,' he said. 'Someone must have been around recently to light the fire.'

Mitchum nodded. Both men looked around before emerging from the shelter of the bushes. The place had assumed an almost ghostly atmosphere. Where were Mulligan and the rest of his gang? Why was the place deserted? Cherokee George bent low, examining the ground.

'Boot prints,' he said.

Mitchum joined him.

'Only one set.'

The whole area was considerably scuffed up. The boot prints led off into some trees and there were clear signs of a horse having ridden away.

'Not long ago either,' Cherokee said.

They looked out into the night.

'We've been duped,' Mitchum said. 'Mulligan isn't the fool we took him to be. He and the gang have gone on ahead of us.'

'Why would he do that?'

'Because he's twigged that we're headin' for Black Valley Forge and aims to get there first.'

They followed the trail of the horse for some distance.

'There's no sign of any other horses. At some point, probably yesterday, they struck off on a different trail. Remember Mulligan knows the country well.'

'That means they could be half a day in front of us.'

'Maybe more. This might not be the first night they've pulled this stunt.'

'And we were thinking we were ahead of the game. This gives 'em an edge.'

'Guess all we can do is move on now as quickly as possible,' Mitchum said.

'Like right now. We'll pick up the rest of our things when we ride past the camp.'

Quickly, they walked back to their horses and stepped into leather.

★　★　★

For most of his waking hours, Turkey Joe's thoughts dwelled on what he conceived as the treachery of Cherokee George. He had brought Cherokee George into his gang and this was how he had been rewarded. He should have known better than to trust the mangy varmint. That was his trouble — he had always been too trusting for his own good. After following Cherokee and Mitchum for less than a day he had worked out in which direction they were headed and the realization that they were aiming for Black Valley Forge only made his thirst for revenge the stronger. Wherever that loot was concealed, it belonged to him and Cherokee George's betrayal was all the more odious in that he was obviously intending to get the money himself. He had no right to it whatsoever. That loot belonged to Mulligan. After all, it was he who had been involved in carrying out the railroad robbery in the first place. It was his by right. He had stopped thinking about the claims of the rest of the gang. He had plans to resurrect the old days, beginning with a stagecoach hold-up. That particular scheme would have to be put on ice. He had lost no time in getting on the trail of Mitchum and Cherokee George but as he rode hard in pursuit of them a new plan began to form in his head. If he could get to Black Valley Forge before them, he would be in a position to have first crack at finding the hidden hoard of money. Almost equally important, given the state of his feelings, he would be able to establish himself in the best possible position to deal with them. Mitchum and Cherokee George would ride straight into the trap he intended to set, and this time there would be no escape for either of them. Leaving one of his men to set up the hoax camp-fires, he turned off the trail he had been following and, accompanied by the rest of the gang, set his course for a cut-off which he knew would bring them by a different route into Black Valley.

*　*　*

Mitchum and Cherokee George continued riding through the night. Just before dawn they stopped to rest the horses and make a hasty breakfast before heading on again. They rode for the rest of that day, taking breaks so that the horses would not get blown. When night had fallen they made camp but were up before the dawn. The hills were becoming more like mountains and the valleys like canyons. Although it was daylight on the peaks, it was still dark in their shadows. Gradually the valley became bathed in light.

'You sure you know where you're goin'?' Cherokee asked.

Mitchum didn't like to admit to his uncertainty. He was pretty sure they were going in the right direction but it was hard to differentiate one place from another. He was looking for a landmark but in the end it wasn't any landmark he recognized which convinced him they were on the right track. They had come round a bend when off to their right they saw sign. A narrow trail intersected the one they were following and, riding up it for some little way, they could clearly discern the tracks of riders coming down it. Rejoining the trail they were following, they could easily pick up the tracks and there were droppings at the side.

'Looks like Mulligan and his boys took a diversion and came back on the main trail just at this point,' Mitchum said.

'That means we can't be far from Black Valley,' Cherokee replied.

Mitchum's brow was puckered.

'Pity we couldn't have got here a bit earlier,' he replied. 'Looks like they've got control of the Forge. We're gonna have to be real careful ridin' in. They'll have men posted at all the main strategic points.'

'Maybe it's just as well,' Cherokee responded.

'How do you work that out?'

'I don't like bein' botttled in,' Cherokee replied. 'I'd rather take my chances this way.'

They had ridden on a little further when Cherokee stopped and jumped from the saddle. He bent down to examine the sign again. He looked up at Mitchum.

'There's not more than half a dozen riders,' he said.

'So what?'

'Turkey Joe would have had more.

There's somethin' else too. Some of these tracks are older than others.'

'What are you sayin'?'

'Judgin' from the evidence, I'd say there were three or four in one group and two in the other.'

'What? The two riders were chasin' after the others?'

'I reckon that's about the size of it.'

Mitchum got down to take a look. He couldn't match Cherokee George's tracking skills and he wouldn't have been able to make the same deductions. He valued Cherokee's ability.

'So if these tracks ain't been left by Turkey Joe and his gang, whose tracks are they?'

'I don't know. They all seem to have been ridin' hard. One other thing. I reckon a lot of these prints were made by mustangs. They have a different way of movin' even when they've been broken in.'

Mitchum was doing some hard thinking.

'Mustangs,' he repeated. 'I think I

mentioned a spread called the Quarter Circle Bucket. They run a few mustangs.'

He was thinking it was a long shot, but if it was Bucket and some of his men, what would they be doing out here in the Moccasins? Was there a tie-in to the shooting of Hayes after all? He couldn't figure it out.

'There's no point in standin' about here speculatin',' he concluded. 'Whoever these prints belong to, Turkey Joe for sure is holed up right now at Black Valley Forge and we need to get there pronto.'

They swung up back into the saddle and carried on down the trail.

7

Black Valley was aptly named. Hemmed in by high hills on all sides, it lay in shadow for a good part of the morning and again in the late afternoon. On the western side the hills were crowned with a sheer black granite ledge and in various places landfalls had created glacis of dark rock and rubble. It seemed strange that anyone should have settled there, but the place was well watered and a number of trails led in and out of the valley, linking it to the rest of the Moccasin range and providing good means of entrance and exit. Because of this the trading post and forge had been established years before and existed for a good long time before becoming abandoned and falling into disrepair. The decaying buildings stood by a tributary of the main stream where various paths intersected, near a grove of trees. It had made an ideal spot for Turkey Joe's gang of outlaws to establish themselves and the gang had become known as the Black Valley Forge gang. Now, sitting his horse and looking down on the scene of his greatest triumphs, Turkey Joe felt a glow of pride and satisfaction suffuse him. He was back at Black Valley Forge and the gang was resurrected. A lot of the old members were together again, along with some new recruits. They were ready to ride once more. All that was needed to make things perfect was to find that long-lost loot. It was his by right and finding it after all this time would serve to cement his position as leader of the gang. Good times were back again.

He turned to the nearest rider, one of the original gang named Wayne Coates.

'Sure feels good to be back,' he said.

'Sure does,' Coates said.

'Things is just gettin' started. Soon it's gonna be just like the old days.'

Turkey Joe turned to the dozen or so riders behind him.

'The loot's down there somewhere at the old forge,' he shouted.

Some of the men began to cheer and throw their hats in the air. A couple of men drew their revolvers and began to fire indiscriminately.

'OK boss, let's get down there and get ready for that stinkin' rat Cherokee and his new found friend Mitchum.'

Turkey Joe turned to Coates.

'This time there'll be no escape,' he muttered.

'What you plannin' to do with them?'

'That's easy. If we don't locate the loot straight off, we torture Mitchum till he's beggin' to tell us where it is.'

'What if we do find it straight off?'

'Then we torture him anyway.'

Coates laughed.

'As for Cherokee George,' Mulligan continued, 'he's gonna die real slow too.'

'Why not get one of his own scorpions to bite him?' someone shouted.

Mulligan's face was twisted with hate.

'Leave it to me,' he said. 'Once I've had my way with him, you can do the rest.'

There was another burst of laughter and hooting.

'OK boys, let's go and make ourselves at home.'

Still shouting and cheering, they rode down to the old forge. It didn't take long. As he approached the tumble-down buildings, Mulligan's eyes were already scanning them for places where the loot might be concealed. The men were excited. They rode into the overgrown yard and dismounted, tying their horses to the leaning hitching posts. They weren't expecting to see any signs of recent visitors and they didn't notice the hoof prints in the grass and the dust which were soon obliterated by their own activities.

'Listen up!' Mulligan called.

The men were still excited and it took a few moments for them to settle down. When they had done so he assigned them areas to start looking for the missing hoard.

'We'll give it till sundown,' he shouted. 'After that, we meet back here. I want to make this place secure so we'll arrange just who is goin' to take up position where. I'll be wantin' a couple of you to ride back up the trail to give the rest of us warning when Mitchum and Cherokee appear.'

'When do we get to eat?' someone yelled.

'Plenty of time for that. I take it you boys don't object to a little treasure huntin' before supper?'

Again there was general uproar and a man standing next to the person who had shouted jammed his Stetson hard over his eyes.

'OK, let's get lookin'!' Mulligan shouted.

The men split up and began to move about the buildings and the surrounding area. Coates and another man entered the store building while Mulligan made his way to the forge. For a moment he stood outside, for some reason suddenly reluctant to go in. He surveyed the face of the building. The wooden boards were grey and bleached by sunlight and the whole structure leaned slightly to one side. The windows were broken and the door hung loose in its frame. He stepped forward and entered. It took a few moments for his eyes to adjust. Inside the place was dusty and festooned with cobwebs. Dust motes swam in the beams of light coming through the window frames and doors. Some old tools lay on the floor and in the middle of the room the old heavy anvil still stood, maintaining a kind of lonely vigil like an old soldier on a deserted battle field. The furnace was split and blackened; a cracked bellows leaned against it. A fireplace still held some crumbling ashes. Mulligan advanced into the room. The corners were filled with shadows and it wasn't till his eyes were fully used to the light that he saw an object lying in the far corner which made him jump. Instinctively his hand reached for his six-gun but the object had nothing to fear any more from the impact of a bullet. When Mulligan stepped forward to take a closer look, he saw that it was a skeleton, the bones still somehow held together by the clothes it wore. Mulligan swore beneath his breath, turned and made quickly for the door.

He stood outside in the sunlight, gathering his wits. He couldn't understand why he felt so shaken. He had seen dead bodies before, plenty of them. He lived in a world of violence where death was the frequent outcome of some minor altercation. He had seen hanged men and ugly wounds and mounds of bones. None of the things he had witnessed, however, had affected him like this. Cursing himself for his reaction, he breathed deeply of the mountain air and went back inside the forge. He approached the skeleton and, bending close, saw that the skull had been caved in at the back by a blow from some heavy blunt instrument or a rifle butt. Gingerly, he touched the man's jacket, feeling for a pocket in the hope of finding some clue to his identity. The shattered skull seemed to turn in his direction and direct a cold, hollow stare at him before the skeleton toppled over, raising a cloud of dust. It was no longer the form of a man but a heap of bones still contained by the frayed and tattered clothes it was dressed in.

Mulligan flinched. He had to fight against the urge to run outside again but he managed to do so. He felt inside all of the man's pockets but they were empty. He stood up and stepped back. Was the skeleton the remains of the blacksmith and livery man? He walked to one of the windows and peered outside. He could see the broken poles of what had been the corral and further back, a grove of trees. One of the outlaws was poking about as if the buried loot might be just below the surface of the corral.

Mulligan breathed the outside air into his lungs once more and faced back into the greyness of the forge. He looked about him, trying to concentrate on the loot rather than the grisly remains in the corner. He began to walk around the forge, checking the walls. It was quite an extensive building. When he reached the fireplace he stopped and bent down to look up into the flu. He struck a match and the blackness of the chimney was flickeringly illuminated to a certain height. He could see nothing like a shelf or a recess but he noted the flu as one likely spot that would merit further investigation. He examined the anvil in more detail and pulled and pushed at it as though it might spring up and reveal some secret passage. He was still feeling shaky and he couldn't give his attention to the task in hand. He decided that it might be better to come back later with some of his men and investigate the place properly. He made his way back to the door. If he had been properly aware, he would have seen the imprint of boots on the dusty floor but in his dazed state he would probably have taken them for his own.

Standing by the door of the forge, he became aware of sounds — the rustle of the breeze in the tree-tops, the call of a bird, and over these natural sounds, the voices of his men and the occasional shout as they called to one another. It was as if he had entered another world when he went into the forge, a closed and remote world cut off from everyday things. It was with a feeling of relief that he reached into his pocket, pulled out his pack of Bull Durham, and built himself a cigarette. He drew the smoke into his lungs and blew it out so that it hung in the air in front of his face. He heard footsteps and the figure of Coates suddenly materialized from round a corner of the dilapidated store building.

'Have you found anythin'?' Coates asked.

Mulligan pointed with his finger into the forge.

'What?' Coates said.

Mulligan did not reply and Coates went through the door. Mulligan drew on his cigarette. After a few minutes Coates returned.

'Some old bones,' he said. 'Looks like he was buffaloed.'

Mulligan turned his head.

'Yeah.'

Coates looked closely at Turkey Joe.

'You OK?' he asked.

At his words something seemed to fall like a weight from Mulligan's shoulders.

'Sure,' he said, dropping the cigarette to the ground and stubbing it out with the heel of his boot. 'Come on. Let's see how the rest of the boys have been doin'.'

★   ★   ★

Bucket hadn't wasted any time. He knew that a bunch of riders was ahead of him and he was sure that it must be Mulligan and some of his fellow

203

gunnies. Taking a short cut through a narrow pass, he rode through the night and emerged into Black Valley just before dawn. He was taking a risk; Mulligan might still have arrived before him, but he didn't think so. There were no horses in the old corral and no sign of recent activity, so far as he could make out through his field glasses.

'Grainger,' he said. 'We'll ride on down to the forge. The rest of you men wait here.'

The Quarter Circle riders were more than happy to take a rest. They had been riding hard for days. Accompanied by his foreman, Bucket galloped towards the old forge buildings. He knew where the money was hidden. Riding into the yard, he dropped from the saddle. Grainger did the same and together they made their way to the forge.

'Wait outside, just in case,' Bucket instructed Grainger.

'Just in case of what?'

Bucket's nerves were on edge. At any

time Mulligan and his gang might appear.

'Just do as I say!' he snapped.

Grainger shrugged his shoulders. Bucket went through the doorway into the old forge. Instinctively, his eyes sought the corner where the grim shape of the skeleton glimmered dimly.

'It was either you or me,' Bucket whispered. 'No hard feelin's.'

The place was dark but Bucket knew exactly what he had to do. Making his way to the opposite corner, he scrabbled around for a few moments close to the floor till he found what he was looking for. Just above floor level, the wood of the wall was marked by what looked like a knot. Bucket pressed hard. At first nothing happened and he cursed beneath his breath. Changing his stance in order to be able to push more firmly, he repeated the action and this time the log gave way to reveal a small cavity. Bucket reached in with his arm. After a few seconds of fumbling his fingers found what he was looking for; a bag wrapped in oilcloth. With a mumbled word of satisfaction, he withdrew the bag and swivelled the section of log so that it fitted perfectly back into place again before making his way outside. Grainger was sitting on the ground, looking towards the hills where the rest of the Quarter Circle Bucket men were waiting. The first rays of dawn were beginning to appear.

'Found what you were lookin' for?' he asked.

Bucket grinned and swung the bag.

'Let's get out of here,' he said.

They quickly made their way back to the horses and climbed into the saddle.

'Ain't you gonna at least take a look?' Grainger said.

Bucket hesitated. He knew the money was in the bag and his nerves were stretched to breaking point.

'It'll only take but a moment,' Grainger added.

'Later,' Bucket concluded. 'Once we're well out of here.'

Without further ado, they began to ride back towards the shelter of the surrounding hills.

* * *

It was early the following morning that Mitchum and Cherokee George arrived at Black Valley. Mitchum took a long look at the forge through his field glasses. He couldn't see anything out of the ordinary. The corrals were empty and the place looked deserted. It was immediately obvious to Cherokee George, however, that Mulligan and the rest of his gang had taken possession of the place.

'They've probably hidden the horses among the trees,' he said. 'They've made an effort to hide any traces but they haven't made a good job of it. The dust in the yard has been swept.'

He was about to hand the glasses to Mitchum when he took them back again. He put them to his eyes and began a long sweep of the surrounding terrain. When he had finished he looked thoughtful.

'You figure the loot is hidden down there somewhere?' he asked.

Mitchum nodded.

'Unless they've already found it.'

'They can't have been here long. Probably arrived sometime yesterday. They'll have had a chance to make an initial search. How would you rate their chances of having found anything?'

'Pretty slim,' Mitchum replied. 'Besides, they'll have spent most of the time getting bedded in and preparing for our arrival.'

Cherokee pointed towards the trees at the back of the forge. They extended back towards a section of the hills which came down at a steeper angle.

'They'll have sentries watching for anybody coming in, especially from this direction. But I figure there could be a chance of us making it to those woods if we climb down from the heights.'

Mitchum looked closely at the hillside.

'Looks mighty steep, especially that top part,' he said.

He glanced about him.

'We could try to locate the guards and take them out,' he suggested.

Cherokee shook his head.

'We don't know how many of them there are,' he said. 'In any case, once we come out into the open we'd be soon spotted from the front of the buildings.'

'OK. Looks like we got some climbin' to do,' Mitchum said.

Taking care not to be seen, they rode around to the point which they reckoned overlooked the woods on the other side. The going was tough as they rode their horses up the steep wooded slope, calculating as best they could the best place to leave them. When the going became virtually impossible they slid from their saddles and hobbled their horses in an open patch surrounded by trees where they could crop the grass. Then, after checking their weapons, they began to move up through the trees.

It was a difficult climb. At various places they were forced to proceed on all fours and the unevenness of the ground, together with the presence of tangled tree roots, forced them to move sideways every so often in order to progress. In some places it was difficult to prevent their feet slipping from under them while in others they sank into a thick carpet of pine needles. After what seemed a long and exhausting struggle they came through the trees, emerging on a bare and stony stretch of hillside crowned by a steep edge of darker rock. While it was not especially high, it offered a stiff challenge to their climbing skills. They scrambled their way upwards till they stood beneath the sheer rock wall. They looked along the edge both left and right but at no point did it fall away to offer an easier way up.

'We could walk along it and see if it drops off at some point further on,' Mitchum suggested.

'Let's take a closer look,' Cherokee replied.

210

They chose to move to the left, which would take them away from where they figured any of the sentries might be posted. After walking and stumbling a short distance Mitchum halted.

'There seems to be a way up here,' he said.

At the point he indicated there had been a fall of rock sometime in the past and it seemed possible to climb up. About half-way up the wall of rock became steeper but it was not as sheer as the other places they had seen. There seemed to be projections and recesses which might offer hand and foot holds. The main difficulty was that the top part was almost vertical. Only a few stunted trees and hanging bushes offered possible support. Cherokee peered up and examined the prospect.

'It's as good a place as any,' he concluded. 'I guess we ain't got much choice.'

Without further ado Mitchum began to scale the litter of rocks left by the landslide. Cherokee was close behind him, content to let Mitchum seek out the best route. The first few steps were easy enough but then the rocks were piled more steeply one upon another. Mitchum had to reach for a foothold and several times he slipped over, grazing his hands and one knee in the process. Carrying the rifle made things more difficult. Struggling for breath, Mitchum reached the top of the rock pile and looked about for the best place to continue the ascent of the edge. Placing his toe on a narrow projection and his hand in a gap, he levered himself upwards. The next step was easier and he made it to a narrow ledge, where he looked down at Cherokee coming up behind him. Cherokee grinned.

'Pretend there's a cougar on your tail,' he grunted.

Mitchum began to climb again, searching for holds and clinging to the rock. Although the rock wall they were scaling wasn't really high, looking down had made him feel slightly giddy and he determined not to do it again. Instead he tried to focus on the next step, which was difficult because his brain wanted to think ahead, about how they would deal with Turkey Joe and his men. His hand slipped and he muttered an oath. The rocks were jagged and sharp and blood began to pour from a cut across his palm.

'You OK?' Cherokee called.

'Yeah. Cut my hand is all.'

The pain seemed to concentrate his attention. He was almost at the top of the rock wall but couldn't seem to find the right hold. Cherokee came alongside him and then veered off to the right, finding a new way to accomplish the last few feet. Mitchum followed in his footsteps, keeping his head erect, fighting the urge to look down. He heard Cherokee's voice above him.

'Swing your leg over to the left. That's it. Now grab hold of that branch and pull yourself up.'

He followed Cherokee's instructions. The branch he was clinging to didn't seem very strong. His palm was bloody and he was sweating.

'One more heave and you're there. Here, give me your hand.'

Mitchum looked up. Cherokee was just above him, leaning out over the edge. Cherokee reached down and Mitchum took hold of his arm. Bracing himself and selecting his final foothold, he swung out. Cherokee's arm cracked with the strain but in another moment it was over and the two of them lay panting on the ground at the summit.

They soon had their breath back. Mitchum had sustained a bad cut to his hand but the bleeding was beginning to stop. They had come out on a comparatively wide ridge which descended gently at first but then fell away steeply. From where they had topped the ridge they could see little of the scene immediately beneath but when they walked forward they could see the forge and its outbuildings below them to their right. They had come out rather further along the ridge than they had anticipated.

'Could be an advantage,' Mitchum said. 'We can work our way down more gradually.'

'Yeah, but there's less cover. We need to get among those trees as quickly as possible.'

With a final look about them, they commenced the descent. Although the mountainside was steep, it was easier going down than it had been coming up. Where the going was particularly difficult, they resorted to slithering and sliding down on the seat of their pants. Patches of vegetation acted as a break and it didn't take long till they reached the treeline. It was mainly pine but scattered among the pine trees were some sycamores and oaks. Up to that point they had a clear view of the buildings below but now they had to calculate the best route to follow. After the sunlight on the bare mountain side, it was dark among the trees and very quiet, the rustling of the leaves only seeming to emphasize the silence. Their feet made no sound on the pine needles. Eventually the trees began to thin and they had a view of the valley below them again. The forge was further away than it had seemed from higher up and before they could reach the shelter of the trees behind the corrals there was an open stretch of ground that offered little in the way of cover. At least, that's how it seemed to Mitchum. Cherokee George had no such concerns.

'There's all the cover I need,' he said.

Coming down the hill, Mitchum had been listening for the sound of horses but he hadn't detected anything. He drew Cherokee's attention to the fact.

'I figure they must be either hidden in those trees nearer the forge, or maybe they're using the old stables,' Cherokee replied.

Mitchum considered the situation.

'You figure you can get close to the forge?' he asked.

'Sure. Nobody will see me. I can guarantee that,' Cherokee replied.

Mitchum reflected on how easy it had been for Cherokee to sneak up on him and Flagg to deposit the scorpion.

'Then here's what I propose,' he said. 'You make your way across that open stretch and get close to the buildings. Find out where the horses are being kept and let them loose. I'll work my way around to the front of the forge. Mulligan and his boys will make a rush when they hear the horses getting away. We'll have them covered. They won't be expectin' anything and with you firing from behind and me in front, they'll panic. They might even think there are more than just the two of us. The only way any of 'em will be able to escape will be by goin' back inside and we can deal with 'em in our own time.'

Cherokee nodded.

'Sounds OK to me,' he said. 'We'll have the element of surprise.'

He grinned.

'Yeah, the more I think about it, the better I like it.'

'There's still the question of those

guards up on the hillside,' Mitchum said. 'Once they hear shootin', they'll soon be on their way.'

Cherokee's grin only grew broader.

'They don't seem to have done much of a job spottin' us,' he said. 'Sure, they'll come ridin' down, probably without thinkin'. In which case we'll be able to pick 'em off.'

Mitchum nodded.

'Give me some time to work my way through the woods,' he said. 'You sure you can make it across the open?'

'You're forgettin' I'm part Indian,' Cherokee replied.

'OK,' Mitchum said. 'Let's do it.'

He moved back up to the trees and began to make his way round the side of the hill. Cherokee watched him go and then, licking his lips, dropped to his knees and started to crawl forward.

★　★　★

Putting down the bottle of Forty-rod he had been drinking from, Turkey Joe

218

Mulligan got to his feet and, crossing the floor of the dilapidated general store, peered out of the empty window frame. He was not in the best state of mind and the rot-gut whiskey did nothing to improve either his temper or his reasoning powers. Despite a thorough examination of the buildings, his men had found no trace of the missing loot. Now he had temporarily abandoned the search in order to be ready for the arrival of Mitchum and Cherokee George, whom he expected to ride into the valley at any time. He raised his eyes towards the hills where he had posted a couple of guards and then looked across the valley.

'Any sign of the varmints?' Coates inquired.

'Nope, but they'll be here before long.'

'You're quite sure about that?'

'It's just a question of waitin'.'

'A few of the boys are gettin' kinda jumpy. Especially since we ain't found that money yet.'

Mulligan turned back, feeling exasperated.

'The boys have got to learn to be patient,' he muttered. 'Once we get Mitchum in our clutches, he'll soon tell us where the money is. Believe me, you can count on that.'

Coates laughed.

'Just make sure you let me have a piece of him,' he said. 'And the other one too.'

Mulligan returned to his seat and took another swig from the bottle.

'You sure all the men are in place?' he said.

'Sure. I got all the strategic points covered. As soon as Mitchum and Cherokee George ride into that yard, they'll be blasted straight out of their saddles.'

Mulligan turned to Coates with an ugly leer.

'Don't be a fool,' he said. 'Remember, the whole point is to get those two coyotes alive. Mitchum knows where the money is.'

'Yeah. It was just a manner of speakin'.'

'Make sure the boys got it drummed into their thick skulls.'

'They know,' Coates replied. 'Hey, just take it easy. Everythin's under control.'

Turkey Joe threw back another slug of whiskey.

* * *

Cherokee George reached the wood behind the forge without difficulty. He moved quickly through the trees, looking out for the horses. When he was confident that they weren't there, he slithered forward once again. As he did so, he heard the sound of a horse nickering. So they were somewhere near. He rounded the corral and made for the ruins of a stables standing a little apart from the other buildings. Once in its shadow, he rose to his feet and slipped inside. The horses were there. He breathed a sigh of relief. He had been right in his surmise. Mitchum's plan depended on setting the horses loose. Was Mitchum in position yet? It hadn't taken him long to make his way to the stable. He decided to wait a while longer. Some of the horses were getting restless so he ducked out of the barn doorway and sat down in the shade, his back against the barn wall. He had no fear of being discovered. His ears could detect the sound of a footstep from a long way off. He looked about him, picking out suitable positions from which to fire down on the forge if it came to a siege. He was certain that the outlaws had not posted any men at the back of the forge. They hadn't counted on anyone coming down the steepest slope and making his way across the open ground. All their attention was focused on the trail leading in from the hills at the front. He scratched his head. The time he had spent with the outlaws had convinced him of their stupidity, but this seemed just too careless. Unless . . .

His gaze swept up the hillside. He couldn't see anything to cause concern but he was suddenly convinced that he and Mitchum had been drawn into a trap. Maybe those sentries hadn't missed them after all. He jumped to his feet. There was no time to lose. He would have to assume that Mitchum was in position. Running into the barn, he began to untie the horses. They were uneasy, tossing their heads and stamping. The first ones to be freed began to make their way to the broken doorframe. Quickly, he carried on setting them loose. Some of them were milling about as though confused but the daylight attracted them and they made their way out through the broken walls as well as the open doorway. It couldn't be long before the outlaws heard the noise and realized something was amiss. He ran outside and began to wave his hat. The horses moved away from him. Then a shot rang out from the trees behind the corral and the horses reacted, beginning to stampede. Cherokee George broke into a run, seeking the shelter of another building. More shots rang out, raising dust. Above the noise of the horses' hoofs he could hear sounds of shouting and then a burst of gunfire from further off. He grinned. Mitchum was in position and firing on the outlaws as they burst from the forge and the general store.

Just then a bullet pinged by him, coming from the building he was running towards. At least one of Turkey Joe's men was in possession of it. Veering off, Cherokee ran hard, twisting and turning as he went. Ahead of him was a clump of bushes and he hurled himself into it as more bullets whined by, perilously close. Taking position, he took aim with the .50 calibre Sharps rifle he carried. It had been awkward to tote around but now it came into its own. He watched the outbuilding where the gunnie was concealed very closely. A further shot passed harmlessly overhead but the instant the man's head appeared in the window, Cherokee's finger closed on the trigger. The Sharps barked and the man fell back. Cherokee George trusted his own accuracy enough to know that the gunnie was permanently out of action. He looked back at the trees behind the corral. Presently a figure emerged, glancing about him. The Sharps spoke again and the man went down. Cherokee figured there might be one more in the woods, but for the moment no more shots came from that direction. Cherokee moved back and carefully began to circle the buildings. He figured Mitchum might need some support out front.

Mitchum was firing rapidly into the bunch of outlaws who had emerged when the first horses came crashing round the side of the store. As he had reckoned, they were taken by surprise and didn't seem to be able to understand what was happening. A couple of them ran straight into the path of the galloping horses and were bowled over. Mitchum had a pretty shrewd idea that they had been passing the time drinking. A lot of them certainly acted that way. His own bullets were wreaking havoc when he became aware that further firing was happening somewhere to his right and above him on the hillside. He began to move away through the trees and then drew to a halt again. Whoever was up there was firing not at him but at the outlaws. He rapidly reloaded and began to lend his own weight to the onslaught once more. At the same moment another burst of fire came from the rear of the forge. The owlhoots who had emerged from that building began to run. A couple of them succeeded in springing aboard the horses milling about among the buildings and began to ride away.

'Cherokee!' Mitchum hissed to himself. 'We got them now.'

There was more fire from the woods behind him but for the moment Mitchum didn't have time to waste wondering who it might be. He was watching the scene in front of him for any sign of Turkey Joe. Suddenly, through the smoke and dust, he saw him. He was running in the direction of the trees behind the corral and vanished behind the forge. Rising to his feet, Mitchum began to scramble down the slope in pursuit. The firing from the outlaws had dwindled to almost nothing. Only a sporadic shot rang out now and again. Mitchum knew that he and Cherokee had won the day as he tumbled down the hillside, hitting the level ground at a run. He was concentrating so hard on getting to Turkey Joe that he didn't see another man emerge from the corner of the general store and take aim at him. The rifle roared and Mitchum felt a sharp pain in his leg. Impelled forward by the momentum of his run, he hit the ground hard, banging his head so that for a few moments he was dazed. When he came to he looked up to see one of the Black Valley Forge gang levelling his rifle at his head. He did not recognize the ugly leering face of Coates.

'At least you're gonna die, Mitchum,' Coates said.

Mitchum thought quickly.

'I know where the loot is hidden,' he replied.

Coates's finger was on the trigger of his rifle but he hesitated.

'I can tell you where it is,' Mitchum gasped.

Coates threw a look around him. It was his last. As he turned back his head seemed to explode like a ripe fruit dropped to the ground and he fell forward to lie in the dirt next to Mitchum. Mitchum heard footsteps running up and prepared for his last moment when a voice he recognized called his name.

'Mitchum. Are you OK?'

He turned his head. It was Marshal Stevens!

'What the hell are you doin' here?' Mitchum said.

'Sure looks like we got here in the

nick of time,' Stevens replied.

'We?'

'Yup. Here comes someone I expect you'll remember.'

After a moment another figure appeared.

'Challoner!' Mitchum gasped. 'Hell, I'm beginnin' to think that all this action has affected my brain.'

'Never mind all that,' Stevens replied. 'Looks like you've been hit in the calf. Let's take a look.'

Mitchum glanced down. His leg was bleeding profusely but it seemed to be a clean wound. Bending down, the marshal confirmed that the bullet had passed through part of the flesh but it wasn't serious.

'Sure as hell hurts,' Mitchum replied.

Stevens tore off his neckerchief and bound up the wound. He made a tourniquet out of Mitchum's bandanna. Suddenly Mitchum remembered Turkey Joe.

'Mulligan!' he gasped. 'He was tryin' to get away.'

He made to get up but fell back again. He looked at Stevens. The marshal's face was contorted into a broad grin.

'What are you smilin' at?' Mitchum said.

Stevens moved behind the prostrate body of Mitchum and, hitching his arms round his shoulder, raised him slightly, supporting him as he did so.

'Take a look,' he said.

It took a moment for Mitchum's eyes to absorb the scene. Dust was billowing and smoke hung in the air. Horses were still moving about. Then he saw two figures. One was Cherokee George. The other, with a Sharps rifle pointed at his head, was Turkey Joe.

'Found him back of the corral headin' for the woods,' Cherokee said. 'Figured he'd miss the party less'n I brought him back again.'

It was clear from his glazed eyes and vague expression that Turkey Joe had had too much to drink. At that moment he keeled over and fell to the ground.

'Looks like the Black Valley Forge gang just lost a leader,' Cherokee remarked. 'Leastways, it would have done if there was still a Black Valley Forge gang left.'

He looked all about him.

'Or a Black Valley Forge, come to that,' he said.

Later that night, Cherokee George, Marshal Stevens and Challoner were sitting in the clapped out store building of Black Valley Forge. Mitchum lay beside them, stretched full length on a blanket on the floor. Turkey Joe and a few surviving members of his gang were tied up and secured in the one building which still had a door to lock, prior to being escorted to the jailhouse at Red Rock.

'So we were right about Bucket,' Mitchum said to Stevens, 'and it was you two who were hot on his trail. We saw your sign. Looks like he beat us all to it. I figure he knew where the loot was hidden.'

He turned to Challoner.

'I would never have figured you for a Pinkerton man,' he added.

Cherokee George looked uncomfortable.

'Seems like maybe I backed the wrong horse all along,' he said.

'Don't be too upset about it,' Challoner replied. 'There's a reward out for recovery of the loot and I'm sure you'll be due a share of it.'

Mitchum groaned.

'But we ain't recovered it. Looks like Bucket trumped us all. Maybe we can catch up with him when we get back to Sagegrease.'

Stevens unexpectedly burst into a laugh. Mitchum and Cherokee George looked at him bemusedly.

'That's just where you're wrong,' the marshal said. 'You see, we have recovered it.'

He moved away, returning presently with an oilcloth covered pouch.

'Here is the money. Mr Challoner found it by a process of close observation worthy of the finest detective. Pinkerton obviously don't choose their agents for nothing.'

'Where was it?' Mitchum gasped.

'It was hidden in a concealed compartment within one of the walls of the forge.'

Mitchum was struggling to come to an understanding.

'Bucket didn't get here first,' Stevens said. 'We did. We substituted a bag containing scraps of paper for the one with the money.'

He turned to Challoner.

'I wonder if Bucket's realized his mistake by now.'

Challoner shrugged.

'If so, he could be back any time.'

'I think not,' the marshal replied. 'He'll realize that somebody made a substitution. He'll assume it was Mulligan or some member of the Black Valley Forge gang. Although he has some of his men riding with him, I doubt that either he or they would have the stomach for a confrontation.'

He turned to Mitchum.

'So, like you say, we can take our time about Mr Bucket and catch up with him in Sagegrease.'

Mitchum and Cherokee George exchanged glances and then they all laughed.

'There's one other thing I need to do in Red Rock, besides handing Mulligan over to the law,' Mitchum said.

'Yeah, what's that?' Challoner replied.

'Collect my friend Flagg. I said I'd meet him at Dutch Pete's. Hell, that must have been days ago.'

Marshal Stevens laughed again.

'I figure old Zachary Flagg will be in his element,' he said. 'He likes to get out and about. He'll be makin' the most of this.'

'He woulda come with me right into Turkey Joe's hideout,' Mitchum replied, 'but I figured it was my affair. We saw some tracks. I made out they could have been made by members of the Black Valley Forge gang.'

'He's a good man,' Stevens replied. 'By the way though, I don't really figure there was much truth to that story he told you about his brother bein' injured in the railroad robbery. I reckon it was more likely his way to try and persuade you to take him along with you.'

There was quiet for a while before Mitchum spoke again.

'You say that Jimmy's dog got injured in that kidnappin' incident you mentioned?' he said to Stevens.

'Yeah, that's right. But he's gonna be fine.'

'Musta been upsettin' for the boy and for his mother.'

Stevens nodded.

'And you're sure they're both OK?' Mitchum said.

Stevens looked closely at the injured man.

'Guess they will be when you get back to Sagegrease,' he said. 'But don't make a habit of only stayin' with Lucy Wetherall when you're hurt.'

'Nope,' Mitchum replied. 'Reckon I owe her a lot more than that.'

Cherokee George had been looking

thoughtful. He stood up and moved to the window, peering out across the dark valley.

'Reckon I got some business in Red Rock too,' he said.

'Yeah? What would that be?' Mitchum replied.

Cherokee George turned back to the others.

'Makin' my apologies to the oldster about that scorpion.'

THE END

SOFT SOAP FOR A HARD CASE

Billy Hall

Sam Heller had been hit — hampered in his speed of drawing and holding a gun. He and a homesteader faced Lance Russell and his trusty sidekick when they stepped out from behind a shed. Two against two, yet Sam didn't have a chance: he would always struggle to out-draw them. Meanwhile, Kate Bond waited, hoping for his return, whilst her beloved Sam was determined to go down fighting. Then Russell and his hired gunmen went for their guns . . .

THE MARK OF TRASK

Michael D. George

Mohawk Flats was a peaceful town in a fertile valley; its townsfolk had never required weaponry. They'd grown wealthy and naïve regarding the ways of the outside world — until the ruthless Largo gang arrived. They discovered an Eden ripe and ready for the taking, unaware that a famed gunfighter, Trask, was hot on their trail. Although ill, he knew what had to be done. Soon the Largo gang would know why Trask was feared by all who faced him . . .

KATO'S ARMY

D. M. Harrison

Wells Fargo Agent Jay Kato didn't want to deliver this consignment of gold. Green River Springs held too many bad memories and his cousin, Duke Heeley, threatened to kill him if he ever returned there. However, misgivings were put aside with the offer of a generous bonus, just to deliver the money to the marshal. But as he stepped off the train, a hail of bullets greeted him. Kato would have to raise an army to fight them all.

THE PRAIRIE MAN

I. J. Parnham

When young friends Temple Kennedy and Hank Pierce, ignored ghostly warnings about the 'Prairie Man' and continued with their daring, nightly adventures, it almost led to a tragic accident. But Hank had saved his friend's life and Temple vowed to return the favour. Fifteen years later, Hank, a respected citizen, is wrongly accused of murder. Temple, now an outlaw, vows to save Hank. However, his investigations lead to a man who isn't even supposed to exist: the Prairie Man . . .